Advance Praise for
Stephanie Lehmann and
THOUGHTS WHILE HAVING SEX

"In her first book, Stephanie Lehmann pulls back
the curtain of low rent theater in New York.
Brooding (but hot) directors, bitchy (but hot)
actresses, intellectual (but hot) writers. It's a story
about the young, talented and ambitious and how
they collide on and off (way off) Broadway. You'll
laugh. You'll cry. You'll applaud."

—Valerie Frankel, author of *The Accidental Virgin*

Thoughts While Having Sex

Stephanie Lehmann

KENSINGTON BOOKS
http://www.kensingtonbooks.com

KENSINGTON BOOKS are published by

Kensington Publishing Corp.
850 Third Avenue
New York, NY 10022

All Kensington titles, imprints and distributed lines are available at special quantity discounts for bulk purchases for sales promotion, premiums, fund-raising, educational or institutional use.

Special book excerpts or customized prntings can also be created to fit specific needs. For details, write or phone the office of Kensington Special Sales Manager: Kensington Publishing Corp., 850 Third Avenue, New York, NY 10022. Attn. Special Sales Department. Phone: 1-800-221-2647.

ISBN 0-7582-0333-0

First Kensington Paperback Printing: January 2003
10 9 8 7 6 5 4 3 2 1

Printed in the United States of America

Acknowledgments

Thanks to my agent Barbara Lowenstein and my editor John Scognamiglio, Also, Miles Lott, David Port, Elizabeth Kandall, Lisa Ammon, Wendy Walker, and Anne Galin. Special thanks to Alix Kates Shulman, who helped me learn to talk about sex, and to my parents, for actually having sex (especially that one particular time). Thanks to Stuart Warmflash and the other writers and actors at the Harbor Theatre for giving me a home away from home. And thanks to Steve, Madeleine, and Dave for giving me a home at home.

Finally, I want to thank some of the many actresses who have given me the thrill of hearing my words acted out on stage. In order of appearance: Patricia Randell, Mary Rose Synek, Karin Sibrava, Terri Galvin, Alicia Reiner, Stacey Leigh Ivey, Jennifer La Corte, and Dee Dee Friedman. I think I'm still speaking with all of them. Also, Barbara, I miss you.

Thoughts While Having Sex

Prologue

I don't go to Broadway plays very often. Orchestra tickets are so expensive. And who wants to sit in the balcony? I don't see the point of going to a play if I can't see the faces of the actors. But I did want to see *Betrayal* at the Helen Hayes Theater because Kelly Cavanna was in it, and I used to know her before she got famous. I had this fantasy that after the show I would visit her dressing room backstage. It would be like in that movie *All About Eve* with Bette Davis, and I'd watch her take off her makeup while a maid hung up her costumes and everyone made wisecracks.

But this was not likely to happen. Because the truth is, we didn't part on the best of terms. And I was still angry over the way she'd treated me. So part of me wanted her to get bad reviews and embarrass herself in front of everyone. I hate that, when I want someone to fail. As if that would make my own life better in any discernible way. Not that my ill wishes came true or anything. She got great reviews and ticket sales were going strong. I tried to feel happy for her, I really did, but it was annoying to see her be so exalted when I knew what she was really like. And then to have to feel jealous on top of that.

Not that I'm an actress too, god forbid. I'm a playwright. And I wrote the play she was performing in when she was discovered by a producer who put her in a Broadway play where she was noticed by a casting director who got her a part in a sitcom which led to her first movie which led to her second movie which led to her being nominated for an Academy Award.

The theater world loses a lot of good people that way. When New York actors get some success they almost inevitably go off to Hollywood. Some people even say that theater is dead. Well, maybe the New York theater world isn't exactly vibrant anymore. But I don't think "theater" will ever die. Because it's so much a part of how we live. Every day is a performance, every conversation is an improv, every fight is a climax, and every sigh of relief is an ending of sorts.

Anyway. Maybe she would've been successful whether she was in my play or not. Who knows. And it wasn't like she was a totally rotten person. I do admire certain things about her. Kelly is a woman who is not afraid of being out there. Both with her feelings and her sexuality. Unlike me. And she inspired me to stop hiding so much. And I guess that's really at the heart of why I want to tell this story.

Chapter

1

Before I ever met Kelly, I'd written a play called *Til Death Do Us Part* that was a drama about two sisters, and I was trying to find a way to get it produced. The Dramatists Guild has a newsletter, and there are always a few theaters advertising for new plays in there. So when I saw the listing for a drama with a maximum of six characters and a simple set to be produced at The Renegade Theater in Chelsea, I circled it. My play only had two characters and it all took place in a bedroom. I'd been sending plays out to theaters advertising in that newsletter for three or four years and nothing ever came of it, but I kept trying. In the theater, Hope Springs Eternal.

And so it was to my great surprise when, about two months after I sent the script in, a guy named Peter Heller called and asked if I'd like to meet for coffee. He didn't say on the phone if he liked the play. But unless he was some kind of sadist with a lot of time on his hands who wanted to tell me how bad it was to my face, I figured maybe he was interested.

We met at the Westway Diner on Ninth Avenue and sat at a booth in the back near a brightly lit showcase of gigantic cakes and pies. I'd been to this place many times and knew their desserts looked much better than they tasted, so I wisely ordered coffee and a bowl of rice pudding. Peter Heller ordered a bowl of lentil soup.

"So what are you going to do with this play?" he asked, after the waiter finished pouring my coffee.

I was disappointed. I wanted him to tell me what *he* was going to do with it. "Well. I'd like to find a way to get it produced. And I'd be interested to hear what you think of it."

"I was very impressed."

"Thank you." I waited for him to tell me what was wrong with it. In the theater, it seems like people always expect you to be rewriting. As if it's arrogant to think you've actually finished something.

He took a spoonful of soup and then said, "I think it's ready to be produced."

We looked at each other, and I tried not to let him see my surprise. I should mention, I thought he was very cute. Late 20s or early 30s. Brown curly hair that gave the impression of being blond. Not very tanned but not pale either. I'm not good at descriptions, but in any case he was very good looking. To me, at least.

"Have you sent it out," he asked, "to a lot of places?"

"I plan to. The Public, Manhattan Theatre Club, Playwrights Horizons . . ." As if just mentioning those theaters would make me sound more impressive.

"Why should you send it to them? They'll just send it back. You have no name and hardly any credits—why should they produce you?"

He'd obviously looked at the resumé I'd sent in with my play. I had two productions to speak of, both comedies. *Reservations for One* was staged at the Stella Adler Studio Theater when I was an undergraduate at Tisch School of the

Arts at NYU. An online review from that production commented that "the playwright was sitting in the back row laughing harder than anyone else." My other comedy, *Reality Check*, was produced by a bunch of friends soon after graduation at a little black box theater on East 4th Street. It ran for two weeks. I pretty much stopped speaking to any of those people after we opened. In any case, *Til Death Do Us Part* was my first drama, and I considered it to be my most accomplished writing yet. But I wanted Peter to see I had no illusions about how hard it is to get a play done.

"They shouldn't produce me," I said magnanimously.

"It's tough to get audiences in to see a play," he went on. "Even one by a well-known writer. So why would they risk five hundred thousand dollars for a first-class production on you?"

"They wouldn't."

"Especially since there's little hope for investors to make that money back."

"It would be crazy," I agreed.

"And that's why you can't take rejections personally."

"Because I should know it's hopeless. And I'm insane to be doing this, and the sooner I go back to school and get a degree in accounting, the better."

"That's not what I'm saying."

"No?"

"I'm saying that it's not a reflection on your talents when you keep getting rejections. And that's why you have to keep sending things out."

"To make my odds better," I said, now trying to sound upbeat.

"And to get them to know you and your writing."

"Because you never know what may happen down the line."

"That rejection letter may be the beginning of a beautiful relationship."

I looked at him and wondered if this was going to be the beginning of a beautiful relationship.

"So," he continued, "you still haven't answered my question. What are you going to do with the play?"

"Send it out to hundreds of producers and theaters all across the country and feel good about getting as many rejections as I can?"

"Once again," he smiled, "you have not given me the right answer."

"Which is?"

"You're going to give it to me to direct."

I was very happy to hear this. But I didn't want to presume too much. "Direct, like, a reading? So you can hear it in front of an audience?"

"No. I'd like to direct a full production."

I tried not to look at him like he was insane. After all, he'd just gone over all those reasons why you'd have to be crazy to produce a play by an unknown nobody like me.

"Nothing fancy," he added. "We're talking about a fifty-seat Off Off Broadway theater on the seventh floor of an office building in Chelsea. Are you interested?"

I was glad to have any chance at all to see my play done. Especially by a cute guy like him. But I didn't want to seem too eager. So I said, very casually, "Yes."

I might add, my heart was beating very fast at that moment and I didn't know it then, but I was not going to be able to fall asleep that night because my mind would be racing with thoughts of him and my play and him and my play . . .

"Good. Then let's say we'll plan on putting up an Equity showcase. It'll run four weeks, sixteen performances, and we can open in about two months. If that's okay with you."

I said, as matter of factly as I could, "That sounds fine."

"So I'll put an ad in *Backstage* for the two actresses."

"Great." An ad in *Backstage*. That in itself seemed like a measure of success. But I had one worry. "I think it might be hard to cast the younger sister."

"Why?"

"It's hard to find an actress who's good at holding things in emotionally."

"You think so?"

"Yes, because holding things in is not what an actress tends to do, or she wouldn't become an actress."

"But if she's a good actress, she should be able to. They aren't playing themselves, just like your play isn't an autobiography."

"I guess," I said.

My play, actually, was extremely autobiographical.

As a matter of fact, my older sister Diana would've been perfect to play the part of Julia, the older sister. But she would've been too difficult to work with. She had a lousy temper. And she was not reliable. And then there was the fact that she might not like the way she was portrayed. Not that any of this really mattered. Because she was dead.

That sounded blunt. I didn't mean to sound so emotionless about it. I guess I've gotten used to saying it without feeling like I have to soften the word. And since her death was so upsetting, I guess I tend to go to the opposite extreme and take the feeling out when I mention it. Which I try not to. So I wasn't sure when I was going to. I knew I would have to mention it at some point, but I guess I wanted to think it could be done casually later. Which is ridiculous. I suppose I like to humor myself that her death doesn't always have to be the most important thing about my life.

But she is dead. That's what she is. Killed herself. Dead.

Peter took out his wallet to pay for the bill. "Don't worry. We'll find your younger sister. Now I can't promise you much more than a budget of ten thousand dollars," he said, leaving ten dollars on the table, "but I think we can do a nice job. The technical demands of the play are minimal. And we'll do our best to get some critics to come."

"Great."

"And with any luck we'll get some Off Broadway or Broadway producers too. Because my goal is to help us get this moved to a larger theater. We want this to be the first production of *Til Death Do Us Part*, not the last. That's how I make my money back, and get a reputation too."

"Thank you," I said, "for having faith in my play."

"Thank you," he said, "for writing it."

I smiled. It felt good to hear that. But still. I did wonder. Why my play? Not because I didn't think it was good. But I had to ask myself why a guy would be drawn to a heavy duty drama about two sisters.

It occurred to me that maybe we should've actually talked about the play to see if he saw it the same way I meant it, to avoid any potential artistic differences. But I sensed that he would do a good job with it. And I didn't want to ruin the positive vibes going. Especially when he stood up, and I saw that he was nice and tall, about six foot one, and a bit slim, though not too slim, just the way I liked. Right then, I couldn't imagine having a problem over artistic differences with Peter Heller.

So it's not surprising that after meeting him, I started having insomnia. Not only because of the giddy anticipation of seeing my play produced. But also the giddy anticipation of watching him direct my play and then taking me home every night after rehearsals and making love to me. He would put my play on its feet—and sweep me off of mine.

Of course, I knew it wouldn't be a good idea to get involved with him that way. In real life it would be important to maintain a working relationship that was totally based on our mutual desire to make the play as good as it could possibly be. But in my fantasies, we were maintaining our working relationship mainly for the sex.

A director, after all, is the ultimate authority figure. He tells everyone what to do. And I wanted that in bed too. I wanted someone who would know exactly how to bring my body to life. Someone needed to, because I didn't have a clue.

At this point (I was twenty-five) I'd only had sex with one person. Marc. And it wasn't even good sex. I know that sounds pitiful and it's really embarrassing to admit. But I couldn't manage to figure out how to do what everyone else seemed to do naturally. And I was starting to wonder if I would ever become a full-fledged sexual person.

I had been with Marc my last three years at NYU. He was a fellow playwright who brought hot and steamy one-acts to our writing workshop. But his ability to fictionalize would turn out to be more impressive than his expertise in the sack.

Not that the relationship was all bad. We did a lot of studying together at Bobst library and drinking cappuccinos at Pain et Chocolat and going to movies and plays when we could get cheap tickets. And there was lots of lying around in bed cuddling and kissing and chattering in baby talk. But as soon as things turned genital, we shut our eyes and became silent strangers who happened to be naked and pressed up against each other rocking in sweaty unison until he came. I don't know where his mind went, but I had an unfortunate tendency to imagine my sister hovering over me, watching the show. She'd be there like a little devil, laughing hysterically and almost screeching, "Look at Jennifer! She's having sex! Who does she think she is? She looks like an idiot!"

In any case, our sex life was doomed. Because soon after we both graduated, Marc decided to come into his gayness. I'd been a beard without realizing it. I suppose it may seem a little odd that I didn't catch on, but I swear, he never had trouble getting an erection. Not that I was the most demanding lover in the world.

After Marc admitted his true leanings, at least I knew our lousy sex had been a collaboration. So I was very intent to see what it might be like with a man who was also actually attracted to me. I was very hopeful that man would be Peter. Unfortunately, it was going to take weeks for the production to gear up.

I was facing weeks of insomnia.

And I was getting hooked on this "non-habit forming" homeopathic "sleep aid" from my local health food store.

Something had to be done. One day on the way home from my word processing job, I stopped in my grocery store to get an avocado and I saw a *Cosmopolitan* on the newsstand by the checkout with a blurb on the cover saying, "Wake up to the Best Way to Fall Asleep!" I don't usually read that magazine. It seemed to assume all its readers were tigresses in bed. But maybe I could get some help with my sleeping problem and a few hints on how to become a tigress along the way. So I bought it.

When I got home, I opened the magazine and discovered the technique they had in mind for a good night's sleep was a nice calming session of masturbation.

I hate that word. Masturbation. It was ruined for me ever since the third grade, when I had a teacher named Mr. Bates. Diana, who was in the fifth grade and knew everything, called him Master Bates. This would always launch her into a paroxysm of belly laughs. I had no idea what was so hilarious, but it stuck in my head for years until I knew what that word meant and it finally clicked. In any case, I didn't feel like the "master" of anything, least of all my own body. And I had never, to my knowledge, masturbated. I know that probably sounds odd, but there I was.

I'm not counting my fantasies, by the way, because they were all in my head and never involved actually touching myself.

The idea of touching myself seemed laughable. Like asking myself out on a date. I didn't really know if I wanted to date myself. I can be pretty annoying.

So this article described how to set the scene for "pleasuring yourself." And it said the release of tension sends you right off to sleep. Added bonus: the only way you can really find out what your body likes is by exploring yourself. So I decided if there was any hope of me becoming a tigress, I should give it a go.

Like the article suggested, I turned the lights down low. It wasn't a bad idea, since my apartment wasn't exactly a "romantic" setting. I lived in a fifth floor walk-up on Ninth Avenue a few blocks from the Theater District in Hell's Kitchen. Sarah, an old high school friend who had lived on the floor below helped me get it (helped me bribe the super). She'd since moved out of New York.

I couldn't blame her for leaving. She'd been a dancer. And she was sick of dieting and auditioning and being rejected by her favorite company because she was too short. So she took some science classes at Fordham and got herself accepted into medical school in Florida. I thought she made the right move, but we'd been like Rhoda and Mary with our separate places in the same building. Who expected her to pull a spin-off? I missed her.

Anyway, even though my apartment was just one room with two windows facing smack into a brick wall, it was a great deal at $650 a month and I knew I was lucky to have it. But still. As my sister was fond of saying with her Bette Davis voice: "What a dump."

So then the article suggested taking a bath. This wasn't really possible for me. My bathroom had an old tub that was only big enough to stand up in. So I took a shower. The article said to light a candle or incense, but I didn't have either of those, so I sprayed some Glade honeysuckle air freshener around the room. Then I got under the covers. I have to say, it did feel nice being naked in bed. But after that point, I found the whole thing awkward.

Everyone knows how people who are together a long time can get tired of their partners and the whole idea of having sex can get kind of boring and they'd really just rather watch TV.

Well, I suddenly realized. *Blind Date* was on. That was one of my favorite shows. I used to get a voyeuristic satisfaction out of watching all those couples figure out if they liked each other while being videotaped on a date. My own evening was starting to seem like a very ill-conceived blind date. I started to resent myself for putting myself through it.

But, I reminded myself, I would never become a tigress if I didn't masturbate. So I steeled myself up to rise to the challenge. I lay facedown on the bed and tried to relax. And closed my eyes. And started to try to stimulate myself with my fingers. And started to get a headache.

That's pretty insulting to get a headache when you're trying to have sex with yourself. But the whole thing just seemed ridiculous. To touch myself so intimately. I felt like I didn't know myself well enough to be so intimate with myself. Right in front of myself. I'd have to know myself better.

I got out of bed and put on some pajamas and told myself that after a long day commuting on the subway and working at my word processing job it was hard to get in the mood and I shouldn't take my rejection of myself personally. Maybe, I re-assured myself, I'll be in the mood tomorrow night (dear). And then I snuggled under the covers and dozed off.

Come to think of it, I did accomplish my original goal. What a relief it was to fall asleep and stop worrying about how I was ever going to become a full-fledged sexual person.

Chapter
2

Auditions for *Til Death Do Us Part* couldn't be at the theater itself because the management of Peter's building claimed it involved letting too many strangers in. So Peter rented a room in an old building near Columbus Circle called Shetler Studios. I arrived full of hopeful anticipation on a sunny Saturday morning and walked up two flights of creaky wooden steps. Searching for our room, I passed a belly-dancing class and another theater group auditioning male actors in their 60s.

And then, down at the end of the hall, I saw five or six young actresses studying their lines (my lines!) and whispering to themselves like madwomen.

I love auditions. Some playwrights hate them, especially at the Off Off Broadway level, where you can get dozens of horrible wannabe actresses doing horrible renditions of your lines over and over and over again. But for me, it's a fascinating chance to see other people suffer exposure anxiety, rejection, and humiliation while I sit in a safe bubble of anonymity.

That probably sounds cruel and sadistic. But I mean it in a respectful way. I'm very in awe of actors. They're so willing to expose themselves in public. Writers may suffer a lot of humiliation, but it's mostly in the privacy of their own homes. Compared to actors, writers are total cowards.

But, I admit, I went inside feeling a little full of myself. Peter was there with Carol, a chubby woman in her 50s who was going to be our stage manager, and they were already setting up a folding table and some chairs. A huge stack of headshots was on the table.

Carol called in the first pair of actresses—a short-haired brunette in a baggy sweater and a fleshy redhead with a belly ring.

The scene we were using came towards the end of the play. Peter chose it because the two sisters are really going at each other. He told the brunette to read Melanie, the younger sister, and the redhead to read Julia.

Melanie: "*I was trying to get you to reassure me. To give me your encouragement to go ahead with the wedding. But you wouldn't do that, would you.*"

Julia: "*If you had that many doubts about the man you were going to marry—*"

Melanie: "*Not him. You! You seemed so upset, and I wanted to protect you, and I guess I even played him down a little because I didn't want you to be jealous. And you took advantage of that and twisted me all up inside and I just couldn't be happy knowing that if I got married it would make you unhappy!*"

Julia: "*So you sacrificed yourself and then you blamed me for your entire life. Because it's so much easier than taking responsibility for yourself.*"

Melanie: "*You think it's easy? Going through life like some kind of deformed hunchback, always trying to stay lower, stay lower, so I never overtake you—so I always let you win?*"

Julia: "*Let me win?! You don't even compete. Because you know you'd always lose. And it's so much easier to wallow around in self-pity than to pull your own weight, isn't it.*"

I couldn't help but wonder, as we sat there, if everyone else wondered if this was based on something that really happened. Which it wasn't. Though it felt like it was.

Most of the actresses were totally wrong for both parts, and we could see it the moment they walked in. And then we'd have to go through the whole audition knowing it was hopeless. They could be twenty years older than their headshot, or attractive in a TV kind of way that looked plastic, or unattractive in a real life way that looked depressing, or they spoke in a brogue or a Staten Island accent or lisped . . . One after another came in, exchanged pleasantries, and murdered the scene.

But we did, by the end of the day, find one actress who seemed like she'd be good for the younger sister. Annie, who looked very adorable in blue jean overalls and had a somewhat boyish voice and shoulder-length curly hair, gave a good reading and then practically ran out of the room saying, "That scene was so intense!"

I love to see an actress get affected by what I write, even if she's just doing it to get the part.

But we didn't find a single actress who seemed even close to being able to carry off the part of the older sister.

When we were done, and Peter and Carol were packing up the room, I went to the bathroom. As I suspected, a spot of blood was on the crotch of my underwear. My period had come early. That was annoying. Luckily, I had one mushed mini-pad at the bottom of my purse. I put it on and joined Peter as he made his way out of the building.

"I'm surprised," I said, as we rode down the elevator. "You'd think there'd be a ton of sexy, aggressive actresses out there."

"It's not so easy. First of all, she has to put across a difficult personality and a quick temper. But we also have to feel her vulnerability. That takes a really good actress."

"Plus she should be gorgeous," I added.

"If we don't find someone tomorrow, I guess we'll have to put another ad in *Backstage.*"

"That would be a drag," I said as the elevator doors opened. But I was pretending. I could listen to my lines over and over again and not get bored.

Peter held open the glass door. "You want to go out for a bite to eat?"

I did. But I was worried about that pad. If my flow came on heavy I could start leaking. "Thanks, but, I have to get home."

"Oh. Okay. See you tomorrow then."

"Bye." I hoped he could see I was wistful. As soon as he turned the corner, I hailed a cab.

I always seemed to get my period on the most inconvenient days. Days when important things were happening and the last thing I wanted was my period. Opening night for *Reality Check,* I got my period. The day I took my SATS, I got my period. If I were an ice-skater in the Olympics, I would definitely get my period the day of the long program.

But the worst day of all that I ever got my period was the very first time it came. I was thirteen years old, and it arrived in the early morning before school. Even though it was not unexpected, it still seemed like an uninvited guest and I was not prepared to look at it or smell it or acknowledge its existence, much less entertain. I felt lucky to be able to dip into my sister's Stayfrees. Diana and I shared a bathroom, and I knew the box well, with its picture of a woman walking carefree on the beach (as opposed to running desperately to the toilet). As I pulled the adhesive off the back of the pad, I did feel proud of my body for doing what it was supposed to. But there had to be a better way.

When I headed downstairs, it felt like a diaper was stuffed up into my crotch. I couldn't believe the world expected me to go around like this. I headed towards the kitchen but paused outside the swinging door. Diana, who was fifteen that year, was screaming. I braced myself. Not that this was anything unusual. But still, her eruptions had a way of jump-starting my adrenaline.

That morning she was unhappy about this boy Nathan who was in our theater group, Rising Stars. (I know the name sounds hokey. But they put on real productions in a small theater on Main Street and god knows there wasn't much else to do during the winter in suburban Connecticut.) Diana's shrink was the one who suggested she try acting so she could "have an outlet for her emotions." After she started going, I wanted to go too. I loved hanging out backstage and working crew. Diana seemed okay about having me tag along—maybe because I was always telling her how good she was. She was cast as Juliet at the time, and this boy Nathan was playing Romeo. His latest crime was telling her she should've been playing the nurse because her breasts (she wore a D cup) had so much milk.

"I'm going to kill him! And then I'm going to kill myself!"

"Calm down," my mother said. "Teenage boys are immature, you know that. Just ignore him."

"Ignore him? Are you stupid? I have to kiss him!"

"Do you want me to talk to Mr. Brillstein about it?"

"No! God! You don't understand a fucking thing!"

"I'm just trying to help."

"I shouldn't have told you."

"What do you want from me?"

"Nothing! Forget it! I hate you!" she screamed. Then she caught sight of me watching. "I hate everyone in this house!"

Before exiting, she grabbed a glass that was sitting on the counter and threw it across the room. Then she stormed out of the kitchen and upstairs. She slammed her bedroom door so hard, one of the paintings in the hall fell off its hook and crashed to the floor.

I wondered why I was included in her slur of the entire household. (Even if I did feel smug that my breasts were a more manageable size C.) As a matter of fact, we'd been getting along pretty well recently. Just that weekend we went, just the two of us, to a movie version of *Taming of the Shrew* with Mary Pickford and Douglas Fairbanks that was playing all the way in New Haven. I'd let myself think that maybe she did actually like me a little.

But now I guessed she didn't. That's how it was with her. Some days she was so depressed, she didn't make it out of bed. Some days she was so high she never made it into bed. Up, down, friendly, mean. You never knew what was coming next.

"Mom? There's something I need to talk about."

She didn't answer. She was picking up the bits of broken glass.

"Mom?"

"Can't it wait?" she snapped.

I clenched my teeth, turned and left the room.

The day got worse. I didn't think the flow would be so heavy. I was sitting in Mr. Carter's geometry class and someone told a joke. When I laughed, it gushed out. I felt it all wet and warm in my white cotton underwear and knew that pad couldn't be absorbing all that blood. I feared it had leaked through to the crotch of my jeans, and I had to wait for class to end to find out. Then I raced (as well as I could) to the school bathroom. The pad was saturated, so I layered some of the rough, scratchy squares of toilet paper on top of it. The rest of the day, I walked around in a state of terror that the entire school could smell my blood and see the blotch of red on the crotch of my pants.

After school I went straight home, intent on taking care of the disaster occurring in my underwear. I went up the stairs to the bathroom.

That's when I found my mother on the floor. Sobbing on the bathroom floor. Cleaning a smear of blood off the white tile floor.

"What happened?"

I thought this must be my mess. I had bled all over the floor and not realized it. But how could I have bled all over the floor and not noticed? And why would my mother be crying? And why wasn't she answering me? Maybe Diana was having her period too. Maybe she was the one who had leaked.

"Where's Diana?" I asked.

My mother stopped wiping the floor long enough to wipe some tears off her face. It seemed like it took forever for her to answer. I broke out into a sweat. It had to be something bad. Really bad. And I was dying to go into the cupboard and get one of those pads.

"She's in the hospital," she finally said.

"The hospital?" My stomach was cramping really bad.

"She'll be fine," my mother said. "She'll be fine. She's fine."

"What's wrong with her?"

My mother looked at me. "You should know . . . Your sister . . . She tried to kill herself." She nodded towards the sink, where there was more blood and a razor blade.

My stomach cramped up even worse and I suddenly needed to double over. I went into my room and sat down on my bed (which made another warm flow of blood gush out) and leaned my chin down to my knees. I hated the way it wouldn't stop coming.

My mother came to the doorway of my room. There was a moment of silence. She was staring into space. I sensed this was my chance. Right then. To tell her. About me. Get it over with. Now. I took a deep breath, about to speak.

She looked at me. There was panic in her eyes.

I let my breath out.

She returned to the bathroom.

I couldn't tell her about my blood. There was too much blood already.

I stood back up to see if it had seeped through to my white bedspread. It hadn't, but I was afraid to sit back down. So I didn't sit again until she finished cleaning the bathroom. Then I went in for a fresh pad and put it on a fresh pair of underwear. Luckily, she still had half a box.

Diana never did get to perform *Romeo and Juliet*. She had to go somewhere called Silver Hill and "get some rest." That's how my parents put it. As if she'd been getting too much exercise.

I had no idea (though she would tell me about it later) that they put her on lithium and made her talk to a shrink, who lusted after her, as every shrink would down the line. All I knew was that everything was very peaceful now that she was out of the house. It felt so nice, not having to worry about how Diana felt. I couldn't help but wish she wouldn't come home again.

The next month, when my period came, Diana's box was empty and there was no way I was going to go into the Woolworths and buy my own. I geared up to tell my mother. But I couldn't decide if I should admit I'd stolen Diana's napkins the last month or pretend this was the first time. I didn't want to lie. But I didn't want to tell the truth. So I decided to write a note.

This is what I wrote:

Me: *Mom, I have some exciting news.*
Mom: *What is it?*
Me: *I just got my period.*
Mom: *Oh! That's wonderful!*
Me: *Thanks.*

Mom: *Congratulations. You're now a woman.*
Me: *Yea for me.*
Mom: *I'll tell your father.*
Me: *Don't you dare!*

It was the first scene of dialogue I ever wrote. I was rather proud of it. I watched my mother read it, and enjoyed seeing her smile as she got to the end. She bought it hook, line, and sinker. Or should I say mini, maxi, and super. She went right out and bought me my very own box of Stayfrees.

The second day of auditions for *Til Death Do Us Part*, I came armed with three supersize tampons. I didn't want anything to interfere with my good time. Unfortunately, it seemed that I was the only one having one.

After we made our way down about half the remaining pile of headshots, Carol started ranting, "I can't listen to another one! This is a waste of time! Don't you *know* anyone who could do this part?"

"If I did," Peter hissed back, "I wouldn't have subjected us to this!"

"It just seems surprising that we can't find anyone," I said, standing up and stretching my legs, trying to appear like I was suffering too.

"We will find someone," he said. "This is a part that any actress would die for. When we see her, we'll know."

"Then can I ask you one favor?" Carol pleaded. "Do you think you can cut them off quicker? Because I can't stand listening to this scene over and over!" She looked at me guiltily. "No offense."

"I understand," I said. "Even I am getting a little tired of my own words." (Not really.)

But when we got down to the last three actresses and no

one stood out, even I was worried. We found three potential Melanies, and we all agreed that Annie was our favorite. But not a single Julia.

I asked if we could take a short break so I could hit the bathroom down the hall. As I came out of the room, I snuck a look at the three actresses who were left. Carol had already given them their sides, and there they were, sitting on the floor of the hall, valiantly speaking the lines out loud to themselves, to the air, searching for their meaning, trying to get it right.

There was a skinny redhead with freckles who looked like she should be in an orange juice commercial. A chunky brunette who would've made a good prison guard at Auschwitz. And a dark-haired woman who looked perfect—to play Julia's mother.

I could see. We weren't going to find our Julia.

If only my sister could rise from the dead. No. I had to get rid of that thought. Even in desperate circumstances I wouldn't have cast her. And then she'd have one more reason to be angry with me. (So it was just as well she was dead?) Of course, if she were still alive, I wouldn't have written the play.

I went into the bathroom thinking how ridiculous this was, because there had to be a million Julias out there! Like . . . like . . . this woman who was right here, in the bathroom, looking in the mirror and applying makeup. This gorgeous pale-skinned dirty blonde. Voluptuous, with a real body with real curves and cleavage and I saw immediately she could be Julia. Even though I'd always imagined Julia as dark haired, like my real sister, I knew this woman could be her. If she could act. If she was an actress.

Even though I knew she couldn't be there to audition for my play because we only had three women left and they were already accounted for in the hallway, I hoped against hope. Maybe she was one of the women who hadn't shown up for an earlier slot, and she was here now, ready for her chance to show us what she could do.

I flushed and joined her at the sink. And washed my hands. And debated whether to ask her if she was there to audition for my play. And dried my hands on a paper towel. And tossed it in the garbage. And walked to the door. And turned around.

"Are you here to audition for *Til Death Do Us Part?*" I asked.

"No," she said. She seemed to be done with her makeup and was admiring herself in the mirror.

"Oh. Sorry," I said.

"For what?"

"Interrupting."

"Interrupting what?"

"Your train of thought?"

She smiled. "You mean the fact that I was admiring myself in the mirror?"

"If that's what you were doing."

"Is that what **you** were doing?" She was still facing the mirror, looking at my reflection.

"Admiring myself?" I asked, confused.

She laughed. "Admiring me."

"Are you an actress?" She had to be.

"Guilty as charged."

"So you're here to audition for that other play down the hall with the sixty-year-old men?"

"Uh huh . . ."

"Well, if you feel like auditioning for us, we're looking for . . ." (how to say someone just like you . . . ?) "someone just like you. So if you're at all interested . . ."

She turned around so she was looking at the real me.

"Where are you doing it?"

"Down the hall. I think it's room 303."

"I mean the play."

"Oh. Off Broadway. Well . . . Off Off Broadway, actually."

"Showcase?"

"Yes."

"No thanks."

"It's a good part. Two-character play, two women. A drama."

She smiled. "I'd love to, but they're running late to see me, and I'm already late for my money job, and this audition has completely fucked up my day."

The way she was pretending to be gracious in a way that told you she was pissed off plus the use of an obscenity—I knew she was perfect. "Do you have an extra headshot with you? Maybe we could set something up for another day . . ."

"Sorry. I just brought one and I already gave it to these jerks I'm auditioning for."

"Oh well. Thanks anyway," I said.

"Sorry," she said. "Good luck."

I left the bathroom and went back to Peter and Carol, who were waiting impatiently so we could get the last three women over with. "I just saw the perfect Julia."

Peter practically leaped from his chair. "So bring her in!"

"She wasn't interested."

"Was she really perfect?"

"Yes," I said with conviction. "She was totally perfect."

Peter started for the door.

"She's in the women's room," I called after him. Was he going to go in? I followed him into the hall, and watched as he barged into the bathroom. I considered going in after him, but at that moment felt like I would be intruding, which is ironic if you think about it. I will always be annoyed with myself for not going in there, because I'll never know exactly what he said to change her mind, but in about one minute he came out and announced, "She's reading for us. Get her a side."

He looked anxious.

"Carol has the sides," I said.

"Well then get the sides from Carol," he said. Like I was too slow, or somehow in his way, and we would lose her if we didn't act fast.

"She's going to read it in the bathroom?"

"Just get them," he said.

I was surprised, the way he was acting, that he didn't just give her the part on the spot without asking her to read. But he didn't. He gave her the part fifteen minutes later after she blew us all away with her reading. As for the last three actresses still waiting out in the hall . . . Peter sent them home. Rudely. Without even giving them the chance to audition.

The actress's name was, of course, Kelly Cavanna.

Chapter
3

It's safe to say that most productions have a honeymoon period. It's characterized by a certain idealization of all the other people involved, a feeling of well-meaning enthusiasm that everything will be conflict-free (unlike the last time) and a certain tension over wondering when and how the conflict will in fact begin.

I was feeling very lucky to get Kelly. At first she turned us down. Her agent didn't want her to be in any more showcases, only paying work. He was sending her out on a lot of auditions for soaps until she could snag something Off Broadway. He convinced her this was not worth her time. So a day after the audition, she called Peter back and turned down the part.

But Peter asked her to read the whole play through and think about it. And she did. And she changed her mind. Peter told me it was because the part was so good. I told myself it was because she wanted to have a fling with Peter.

In any case, one thing that made it easier for her to commit was the fact that she could leave any time. It's built into the showcase contract that if an actor is offered paying work during the run of the show, she has the option to leave. And there's nothing you can do about it. Which leaves you totally in the lurch. Because at this level, where you don't pay, it's impossible to get someone to understudy. So you are, in that sense, totally at the mercy of your actors.

We went ahead and cast Annie opposite Kelly even though they weren't that great a physical match sisterwise. Annie was taller than Kelly, which bothered me. I saw Julia as towering over Melanie. Never mind that I had in fact been taller than Diana. I still didn't think of myself that way. Also, Annie was dark skinned with brown hair and Kelly was light skinned with blonde hair. But, as Peter assured me, it's more important to have two really good actresses rather than cast on the basis of looks.

Just the five of us (the two actresses, me, Peter, and Carol) would be at rehearsals. As the Stage Manager, it was Carol's job to keep track of any line changes and record all the blocking in a master script. And, as the actresses started to get off script, she would feed them their lines when they forgot them. It's one of those thankless, unglamorous but totally important jobs.

Our first rehearsal would be a simple read-through of the play. I was running late that afternoon because I couldn't decide what to wear. After trying on almost every piece of clothing I owned, I finally settled on some flared jeans from Express and a powder blue zipper-front T-shirt from Urban Outfitters. Then I had to rush to the subway. It was only a two stop ride, but I figured it would be faster than a cab.

As I stood on the edge of the platform, I paced back and forth. I thought about how odd it was to be on my way to a rehearsal for my play that was being done in New York City. My play about my sister. Who was dead. And I was happy. Because I was having my play (about my dead sister) done in New York City.

Sometimes I felt surprised that I ever did move to Manhattan. Not only because it was intimidating. But also because I voluntarily situated myself in the same city as Diana. It would've been liberating to live on my own somewhere free of all younger sister constraints. But we were both drawn for the same reason. If you wanted to work in the theater, you had to be in New York. And both of us, by the time we were in high school, were theater junkies.

My first two years in high school overlapped with Diana's last two years. The drama teacher, Mr. Flint, put on incredibly ambitious productions of both classics and musicals. Mr. Flint had an aura because he used to direct plays Off Broadway. He probably (I realize now) felt like an utter failure because he ended up in Connecticut teaching high school. But he loved Diana. By the time she was a senior, Diana starred in *Follies*, *Three Sisters*, *The Music Man*, and *Mrs. Warren's Profession*. (How many aspiring actors have their best parts in high school or college because once they try to break into the professional level they can't even get an audition?)

Diana was on lithium then and she was more or less stable. Her mood swings didn't seem much more extreme than many leading ladies under the pressure of carrying a show. In any case, Mr. Flint tolerated her temper tantrums. I suppose he had his own fantasy that she would become a movie star one day and thank him from the podium as she accepted her Academy Award for Best Actress.

I accepted my own role as Best Supporting Sister with grace. I constantly reassured her about how pretty and talented she was. And tried not to let her see how shocked I was when she described giving a blow job to the guy who played Buddy in *Follies*. And comforted her when he dumped her for one of the showgirls. And didn't tell my parents about the pot. Or the parked car she bashed in when she borrowed my father's car. Or the birth control pills from Planned Parenthood. Or the guys she was sleeping with, not even the lawyer who was married. Plus, I was a really good listener. And I gave her as much wise advice as I could based on having no actual experience of my own.

We spent hours at Larry's Diner (which is no more) near the train station talking and drinking sugary coffee and eating creamy cheesecake (it was the only good dessert they had— the pies were made with canned fruit). I felt honored when she confided in me. And wanted to hang out with me. Because Diana, when she was happy, was a lot of fun. (It worried me that I had left that out of my play. That I only portrayed her as the evil older sister. For some reason, when I thought about writing a scene showing her good side, I would suddenly get very tired.)

But Diana could be full of a wonderful exuberance. The way she could slip in and out of characters, break into song, do accents. And she seemed to know everything about makeup and clothes and accessories. In a generous mood, she might give me a mud mask or put my hair into french braids. Once she even gave me a pedicure. Sometimes, I loved being her younger sister.

I just had to make sure not to ever want what she wanted. The one time I can remember being in direct competition with her, it was disastrous. I dared to try out for a Rising Star production of *The Glass Menagerie*. It seemed to me that the part of the ultrashy Laura was all wrong for Diana and just right for me. Diana wasn't even going to Rising Stars anymore—she was too busy with Mr. Flint's productions. And I was curious to see what it would be like going up on stage. But as soon as she heard what I was doing, Diana wanted to try out too.

When we were getting ready for our auditions, Diana pretended everything was cool. We even ran lines with each other, taking turns at being Laura. She probably didn't imagine that I might actually get the part.

I got through my audition in a numb state of terror, full of self-doubt and like I had no right to be there. Diana, the seasoned veteran, owned the stage with confidence.

The next day we were at the theater hanging out on stage with the others to hear who got cast. Mr. Brillstein announced that I had the part of Laura. (I suppose I was a good argument for Method acting.) I looked at Diana to see how she would take it.

At first she laughed this big belly laugh and I thought she was going to be okay. "You cast Jennifer? She can't act. She can't even pretend to act!"

Mr. Brillstein said he thought I would do just fine and a few people clapped for me. That's when Diana started screaming. "You want to screw up your play? Fine! This is why I don't come here anymore. I hate this fucking place!" She was in such a rage, she stepped backwards and fell off the stage and sprained her ankle. I can still remember how she cried with pain and I felt her humiliation. The next day I turned down the part, wondering why I ever let myself consider crossing that boundary.

I told myself it was just as well. Performing would've been nerve-wracking. And I had my sights set on being a writer, anyway.

Of course, high schools have even less need for original plays than Broadway. So I continued to work on crew just to have a reason to hang around the drama department. There were advantages to staying behind the scenes. All the backstage melodramas were highly entertaining (especially when they didn't involve me). And I could safely watch everyone else freak out about getting in front of an audience. I knew I would eventually have my moment. Because in the end, actresses only get to say the lines the writer has given to them. The ultimate power, it seemed to me, was deciding who says what.

I would learn later that actresses have their ways of getting around that. As a matter of fact, Kelly would be my biggest challenge. But I had no premonitions, that first day of rehearsal, of any trouble to come.

A train finally pulled into the station. The doors parted, I nabbed a seat and we sped through the tunnel. There's something about racing underground on a grimy, gritty subway train—I couldn't help but feel like I was finally living a cool existence. (Especially since no one knew how lousy my sex life was.) In high school, I never felt cool. Diana was cool. Especially her senior year, when she played Adelaide in *Guys and Dolls* opposite Nick Englander, the school football star. I was on follow spot, so I had the honor of illuminating her when she danced around half naked on the stage in a little pink cat suit in the Hot Box Girls dance number.

Not surprisingly, lots of boys lusted after her. "Fiddle-dee-dee," I can still hear her saying. She liked to talk with a southern accent like Scarlett O'Hara. "I was up all night trying to decide which boy should take me to the prom." She ended up going with Nick, wearing a very low-cut emerald green formal. I suppose I was jealous. But at least all that attention made her easier to live with.

The train finally reached 28th Street and I bolted into the station and up the stairs and down Seventh Avenue to 26th Street. The Renegade Theater was in the middle of the block in a smallish turn-of-the-century office building about ten floors tall. I took the elevator up to the seventh floor, and the doors opened directly onto the small "lobby" of the theater. The "lobby" was just a space about ten feet by ten feet painted white with an old sofa against the wall.

I rushed into the theater. The others were already there, so I sheepishly said my hellos and took a seat at the table that was set up on stage and tried not to heave from my little sprint. This was the only time I would sit with them like that.

For the rest of rehearsals I'd be in the back row of the theater trying to stay out of the way as much as possible.

Peter introduced the play. *"Til Death Do Us Part* by Jennifer Ward." And the actresses began to read.

Julia: *"So how do you like your new apartment?"*

Melanie: *"It's small. No view. The ceiling is low. It never gets a drop of sun. And I've already stepped on two cockroaches. It's the epitome of Hell's Kitchen—"*

Julia: *"Glamour!"*

Melanie: *"I was going to say grunge. I never thought I'd feel lucky to live in a place with bars on the windows."*

Julia: *"That's the good kind that you can slide open if there's a fire. An accessory every young lady should have."*

As I sat back and recovered from rushing down there, I looked around the theater. Peter had shown me around once, but I hadn't really taken it all in.

One thing I really liked was that even though the theater was far from fancy, it was very new and clean. All the walls were freshly painted white, and the stage floor was jet black. I was disappointed that the seats were just metal folding chairs, but they did sit on risers and were nicely raked.

Melanie: *"You aren't mad at me, are you? Because I'm not staying with you?"*

Julia: *"Of course not. You need your own place. It's Mom and Dad who wanted you to keep an eye on me."*

Melanie: *"You're the one who's going to have to keep an eye on me. This city intimidates me, and I don't know a soul."*

Julia: *"Don't worry. Manhattan is the easiest place in the world to meet people. And no matter how many enemies you make, there's always a fresh supply of unsuspecting people to take their place."*

Everyone chuckled at the truth in that line. I couldn't really take credit for it. Diana once said it to me. She certainly made her share of enemies after moving to New York. Right after graduating from high school, she found a share in the East Vil-

lage and dove right into taking classes and going out on auditions. She was sure she didn't need any college because she
was going to be a star. Period. By the time I followed two years
later, she'd already gotten kicked off a showcase for being a
diva in rehearsals and alienated a string of actor friends and
roommates.

I had known I would be walking straight into the fire. But
told myself Manhattan had to be big enough for both of us.
And I suppose I figured she would need me around when
things got worse.

Julia: *"You really have to develop a thicker skin, Melanie, or peo-
ple are just going to take advantage of you."*
Melanie: *"I know."*
Julia: *"And you have to think positively if you want to get any-
where in this world."*
Melanie: *"You're right. I know. Theoretically."*
Julia: *"Now I want you to repeat after me."*
At this point Julia goes to a window (which someone would
have to build), puts her head out and screams.
Julia: *"I am ambitious!"*
Melanie: *"No."*
Julia: *"Say it! Go ahead."*
Melanie: *"This is really idiotic."*
Julia: (yelling) *"I am ambitious!"*
Melanie goes to the window then and calls out.
Melanie: (without conviction) *"I am ambitious."*
Julia: (yelling) *"And I deserve to succeed!"*
Melanie: *"Do I have to?"*
Julia: (yelling) *"I deserve to succeed!"*
Melanie: *"I deserve to succeed. I suppose."*
We all chuckled, because Annie said it so glumly. She re-
minded me of me.

As they continued on, I thought back to the day my sister did actually try to get me to yell out a window. We were in her apartment, not mine. She wanted to celebrate because she'd had an audition for an Off Broadway production of *The Skin of Our Teeth* that day. She was sure she would get the part of Sabina, the sexy maid. "We'll get dinner anywhere you want as long as it's expensive."

"Don't you think you should wait until you get the part before you celebrate?"

It was highly unlikely, with her lack of credits, that she'd get it. She was lucky to get the audition.

"You have to think positively in this world if anything is going to happen."

"But you don't celebrate before you actually get what you're celebrating for."

"Optimists succeed. Pessimists fail."

"That's what they say."

"Come here. I want you to repeat after me."

She went to her window, opened it up and screamed, "I am ambitious!"

"I'm not doing that."

"Come on," she said, sticking her head out the window again. "I am ambitious! And I deserve to succeed!"

"No way. Forget it."

"I'm getting that part," she said. "You'll see."

"I hope you do. And then we'll celebrate, okay?"

But we never did. Because she didn't get the part. And there was nothing to celebrate.

I tuned back in just as Annie and Kelly reached the end of the first scene.

Julia: *"Why don't you come over to my place later? We'll order in some Chow Fun and rent a movie."*

Melanie: *"My own apartment in New York City. This is going to be so fun."*

Julia: *"Here's an extra key to my place, by the way. In case I ever lock myself out. You're my insurance policy."*

Melanie: *"Good idea. I'll make you an extra key for my place too."*

Julia: *"My little sister. My most favorite person in the world. I'm so happy you're here."*

Diana actually said that to me when I moved to New York. "My most favorite person in the world." I could still hear her saying it. "I'm so happy you're here."

The actresses continued on through the rest of the play. They were doing an excellent job. In the last scene, which takes place after Julia has died, it was so heartbreaking I shed a few tears. I even saw Annie shed a few. If they did this well in performance, the production would be a success.

Not that I had any inflated ideas in my head. The lack of splash generated by my first two modest productions had been humbling. I was beyond assuming the world owed me a chance to make it. And I was not going to be overly optimistic like Diana. So it was way too soon, I cautioned myself, to celebrate.

Chapter

4

About one week into rehearsals, Peter asked me if I'd like to get a bite to eat. "I think it would be good for us to talk about where we're at so far."

"Sure," I said, delighted but nervous at the idea of being alone with him.

We went around the block to Rosie O'Grady's, a pseudo-Irish bar with huge TV screens on all the walls, each one tuned to a different sporting event. We settled into a booth and he asked me, "So how do you think it's going?"

"I just have one worry. Sometimes Annie doesn't seem to be turning the heat up enough. Melanie has to be a match for Julia or the audience will lose interest. She can't be totally dominated by her."

"I noticed that myself. But it's too soon to worry. I'm sure she'll find her way there."

"I'm just glad to hear that you agree."

"Especially in the last scene," he said. "That's her big moment of catharsis. The whole play hinges on her reaching that moment."

I felt relieved. I was in safe hands. He would make sure the play would be realized.

We ordered some food and talked about publicity and the horrible task of getting audiences in and printing up postcards and getting press. For a theater this size this was all done on a small scale, but it still had to be done. Carol was getting students from NYU to help out with lighting and props and box office. Mind boggling to think of all the people involved to make a play happen.

"I hope you approve of what I'm doing so far," Peter said, after the waitress left us a huge plate of curly fries.

"Of course I do."

"I just wanted to make sure. Sometimes it's hard to tell what you're thinking."

It hadn't even occurred to me that he might be feeling insecure about his work.

"I think you're doing great." I dipped a fry in some ketchup. "I know it's going to be really good."

"Good."

"I thought that was obvious to you," I said. "I always think I'm totally transparent."

"That's probably why you work so hard at hiding things." We both smiled at that.

"Except in your writing," he added.

"But you should know . . . I want you to know . . . I feel really good about the fact that you're doing this."

Not for the first time, I wondered why he *was* doing this. What had attracted him to this material? A sibling who had died? Something equally upsetting? "You know that I feel lucky, don't you? That you picked my play?"

He looked pleased. "Now I do."

"Can I ask . . . why you did?"

"Pick your play?"

"Yes. I mean, beyond thinking the writing was good. I'm sure lots of the plays you get have good writing . . ."

"Not as many as you might think."

"But you must have some kind of personal connection to it."

"Yes, I do. Of course I do."

I waited for him to go on, not sure if he would.

And he said, "You're very pretty. Did you know that?"

"Me?"

"Yes."

I realized that whatever the reason was, I wasn't going to find out. At least not then. "Thank you."

"You're welcome."

"Kelly," I said, "is so incredibly beautiful, don't you think?" As soon as I said that, I wished that I hadn't. It slipped out.

"I suppose she has a conventional sort of beauty, but it doesn't really appeal to me."

"I don't think it's conventional at all!" I said, still wondering why I was championing the cause of her physical attractiveness.

"Someone like that," he said, "who knows how beautiful she is—she reeks of herself. She exists so that everyone will admire her. She has to have all the attention. I find that very unattractive."

"I don't think she has to have all the attention. I think she just gets it because she *is* so attractive. As a matter of fact, it probably bothers her to always be looked at like that."

"Why are we talking about her?"

"Because I brought her up."

"Because I told you how pretty you are. And it made you uncomfortable."

"Yes."

"Would you like to go to a movie?"

"Now?"

"Let's walk to the Angelika and see what's playing."

"Okay."

It was wonderful getting to sit right next to him for a whole hour and a half. Occasionally, our shoulders rubbed. I wasn't sure if this was something he deliberately made happen, or if I was making it happen, or if it happened by itself, or some combination of all three. But each time, I felt this jolt through my body. Desire. I wanted him. It scared me.

All through the movie I kept salivating. And I felt like he heard me swallowing so he knew that I was salivating, so he knew that I wanted him. And I didn't want him to know my body was capable of such bodily excretions, because any evidence of stimulation suggested that I was capable of losing control, which was not to be desired, because loss of control seemed downright dangerous.

I hate the word salivating. It makes me think of salamanders, which make me think of tongues, which I don't like to think about. It's odd having this slab of meat in your mouth.

In any case, my mouth kept watering during the movie.

And then he walked me home. On the way, I wondered if he might invite himself up to my apartment, and if he did, would he want to have sex, and what would I do if he did, and how would that interfere with the production . . .

At the entranceway to my building he said, "Well, good-bye."

"Bye. Thanks," I said. When I'm nervous I tend to thank people even if there's nothing specific to thank them for.

"Thank *you*," he said, a slight smile on his face. I thought he was going to kiss me right then. But he didn't. He started to walk away. Then he came back. Then he kissed me. Lightly, on my cheek. We were both blushing so much, it was a relief to be alone again.

I walked up the five flights to my apartment. But I was so light on my feet, the stairwell might as well have been equipped with escalators, because I flew up without any awareness of where I was.

But as soon as I faced my room . . . my little box of a room with four walls two windows and nothing but a TV set to cozy up to . . . I wondered how I would get through the evening. If only Sarah hadn't moved to Florida. I needed her now. It was only 9:30, and I was too revved up. I would have to go out walking, or something. Something.

So before going back out, I went to the bathroom and then checked my machine. There was one message. I played it back, thinking crazily that maybe it was Peter even though I'd just left him. A woman's voice started to speak. "Hi there, it's Kelly. I just came from the gym and I don't want to go back to my apartment for a dreadfully boring evening so I'm wondering if you might like to get coffee with me. Give me a call. Bye."

I felt a little thrill at getting this message from her. Flattered that she was interested in my company. She seemed like a mystery to me, and I longed to know her secrets. I was ready to think she knew everything about the world and how to get anywhere in it.

So I immediately called her back, and we arranged to meet in an Italian café in the West Village for coffee.

It was good to get back out into the hustle of the night. As I snaked my way through the throngs of people in Times Square to the subway station, I thought, this is why I came to New York. I wasn't referring to the assault of noise and weirdos and traffic that existed right outside the haven of my apartment. I wasn't even referring to the plush Broadway theaters that were all within blocks of my doorstep. (Broadway was too much of a long shot—I couldn't let myself take it seriously as a possibility.) I was referring to the fact that I loved hanging out with actresses. And there was an endless supply of them in New York City.

I got off the train at West 4th and walked to Bleecker Street. The bakery, which I'd been to once before, had rows of fruit covered pastries in the window. I stepped inside the brightly lit shop. Kelly was already there. I felt honored to have the chance to sit across from her. She was so beautiful, no matter what Peter said. There was no question that every heterosexual man in sight wanted her. I couldn't even be jealous. Just proud to be the one who got to be with her.

We both ordered coffee and then Kelly suggested we order a piece of cheesecake.

"Cheesecake?" I said.

"They have this incredible ricotta cheesecake here."

I didn't mention about how my sister and I used to eat cheesecake at Larry's Diner. I hadn't eaten a piece of cheesecake since she died. "How about some assorted butter cookies?"

"That's too boring. How about one of those big pieces of chocolate cake?"

I have to say. There is something wonderful about an actress who will eat cake. Most of them are always starving themselves and even though they'll pretend to look twice at some tempting thing smothered with buttercream frosting, their ambition tells them they would be fools, and it's hard enough out there without being a fool.

Not Kelly. She surveyed the glass showcase with intent to consume. "That one with the big pink flower on it . . . it looks totally sinful."

"Sounds good to me."

To make it even more sinful, we both got tall glasses of lattes, and I didn't even ask for lowfat milk since Kelly didn't. The waitress took our order with a conspiratorial smile, and then Kelly leaned forward onto the table. "So. I wanted to tell you how good I think your play is."

"Thank you," I said.

"Good" was not the prize word. Great, wonderful, fantastic would be more like it. But still, praise from her was like, well, buttercream, and I savored it.

"It's not often," she went on, "that an actress finds such a meaty part like Julia."

"I'm glad you feel that way because I know your agent wanted you to get a part on that soap."

"He can take that soap and shove it up his ass," she said, flicking her hair behind her shoulder.

I smiled at her evil grin. If I had an agent, I would be so grateful, I'd probably do everything they told me.

"It's tricky," she said. "You kill yourself to get an agent to represent you, and you want them to help you get parts, but they've just got their eye on the dollar. They don't necessarily have your best interests at heart."

"Yes," I agreed. "It's absurd."

Everyone always complained about their agents. But if you didn't have one, you were desperate to find one. As if when you got one, they would legitimize your entire life. Having an agent was proof that you were a marketable commodity—and isn't that all any of us want to be? A good product?

I once had an agent. Sort of. He was actually an assistant to a real agent. He sent a play of mine out to three theaters. They weren't interested. Maybe they even told him it was terrible. Because then he stopped returning my calls. It was over a year since we'd spoken. So I figured he wasn't my agent anymore.

"But the fucked-up thing is," Kelly said, "my agent asked me out on a date."

"That's creepy." I was jealous. My agent had never asked me out on a date.

"It was disgusting," she went on. "He'd just spent half our meeting talking about his wife, who is dying of cancer, and then he had the nerve to ask me out."

"That is so disgusting!"

"I hate him. But he has some good contacts so I can't dump him yet."

"Has he gotten you any good auditions?"

"*The Importance of Being Earnest* at the Roundabout."

"That's good."

"And something Off Broadway that opened and closed in a week. Thank god I didn't get that. The playwright got totally trashed. Too bad, cuz he seemed like a nice guy."

"I live in fear of that happening. I don't know if I would be able to go on."

"You'd feel like shit for a few weeks but it would pass."

"A few weeks?"

"Okay, a few months maybe, but you'd get over it. You're a resilient person."

I was aware that she didn't know me well enough to know if I was resilient or not. Though hearing her say that I was made me feel like I could be. In any case, it was pretty unlikely that we would get reviewed. We maybe had an outside chance with papers like the *Village Voice* and *Time Out*. But the *New York Times* rarely reviewed a showcase. And Peter's theater didn't have much of a reputation. And it was unlikely his publicist would have much success getting anyone down to see it. But the possibility still loomed enough to make my stomach curdle at the thought.

"So," Kelly leaned forward. "I wanted to ask you something."

"Yes?"

"I've wanted to know, ever since that first day, when I auditioned . . ."

I looked at her, my eyebrows raised.

"And," she continued, "you absolutely do not have to answer me if you don't want to . . ."

"Okay . . ."

"And I really have no right to ask . . ."

"What is it?"

"Your play . . . Is it about you and your sister?"

"What?"

"Is the play about your real sister."

I blinked. "Not really."

Just then the waitress came with the cake.

"Here you are, ladies. And two forks."

Ladies. As if we weren't about to pounce on that piece of cake like two rabid dogs mauling a piece of mutton.

"Thank you," we both said, and Kelly immediately started in.

And I was about to.

But my mouth felt dry. I didn't like it that Kelly had asked that question. I sipped my coffee. Now I wished we'd ordered pie. At least the fruit would've had some lubricating qualities.

But if I didn't act fast, Kelly was going to eat the whole thing. She was eating with gusto. I was impressed. Not one word about how she shouldn't be doing this or how she'd have to work if off later or go the whole next day without eating. I couldn't help but wonder if she was bulimic. I don't mean to say that she was, or to start any dirty rumors. It's not like I ever caught her in the act. But with actresses who have great bodies, you can't help but wonder, when you see them eat cake, what happens to all that buttercream.

"Better have some before it's all gone," she said.

"I guess I better." I took a bite. It was good. I took another.

"I know I'm being nosy," she said, "But I can't help but wonder how much of the play is true," she went on, "because it's . . . I'm sorry . . . but it's just so sad."

This was not what I wanted to hear. And not what I wanted

her to be asking. It was clearly out of bounds. An actress should never care what's "true" and what's "not true" about a script, and a writer should keep her mouth shut about it. And I didn't want to hear that my life was sad!

"The play is fiction," I said.

"I know. I didn't mean—"

"Made up. Nothing that happened in that play happened in real life."

"It's just so—"

"All the action and dialogue are imagined."

"—devastating. The relationship between the sisters. I find it fascinating. I'm sorry if I'm being obnoxious. It just made me so curious to know about you. That's all. But you don't have to tell me anything, of course."

"I will say that the emotional journey that she takes . . . in the play . . . that is true in the sense that I have felt all those feelings. But none of the events happened. Well. Except . . ." I laughed a quick, nervous laugh before continuing. "I did have a sister who died. That did happen."

She looked at me suddenly with such compassion and pity, I felt like I was going to cry.

"I'm sorry," she said.

Don't cry, I commanded myself.

I was not going to cry.

People die all the time.

It was not that big a deal.

Don't you know that by now?

It did not have to be such a big deal.

I hated it—that it was still affecting me like this.

"Can I ask," she asked, "how it happened?"

I eked out a smile. "Not like in the play."

I felt like she was trying to trap me. I reminded myself I didn't have to tell her anything. Not a thing.

"I'm sorry, I'm being incredibly insensitive."

"No—"

"We hardly even know each other."

"It's fine—"

"And here I am trying to worm my way into your private life."

"It's nothing, really."

I looked at the cake. I'd lost my appetite. She must've read my face. "Do you mind?" she asked, her fork poised.

"Go ahead, please," I said, though at that moment eating all that butter and sugar seemed sort of obscene.

She took a generous bite. "I have such a sweet tooth. I really shouldn't. My agent says I have to lose ten pounds."

"I hate your agent."

"Me too." She laughed and took another bite, and I saw chocolate buttercream on her tongue, on her teeth.

"I think it's so wonderful that you don't starve yourself," I said, glad to change the subject.

"You probably think I'm bulimic," she said, taking the last bite—the pink buttercream rose.

"No I don't."

"Well I'm not," she said. "If I were, I'd make myself lose ten pounds."

"You look great just the way you are."

"Thank you. And you know what? I think so too."

I raised my eyebrows in amazement. "A woman who likes her own body? Someone should put you in the Smithsonian."

"You don't like your body?"

"Are you kidding? My hips are too big, my thighs are too fat, and my skin is too white."

"You have a great body."

"Not if you saw me naked."

"You'll have to show me sometime. Let me judge for myself."

I laughed and she smiled and I blushed a little and I

thought how this was just like we were actually flirting with each other. I felt like . . . having a piece of that cake. Too bad it was gone now. I took a long sip of latte. And then I decided to tell her.

"My sister," I said quietly, "she died four years ago. She killed herself."

Kelly looked at me, suddenly quiet. "How?"

"Drug overdose."

Diana had once told me, jokingly, that she would never do herself in by cutting again—it left such unsightly scars (ha ha).

Kelly's face made me tear up again. The sympathy. I hate that sympathy. It was right there next to pity. Sorrow. Horror. Dread. It was right next to *Please God don't let something that bad happen to me.*

As if it was my fault. It wasn't my fault that she died!

"How old was she?"

"Twenty-three."

"God."

"I was twenty-one."

"I'm sorry. I'm so sorry."

We both stared down at the remains of the frosting and crumbs left on the plate. I wondered if she would ask me more. Most people didn't. Too uncomfortable.

"Did you see it coming?" she asked.

In other words, I thought, did you know she was suicidal but failed to do anything about it?

"She had a history of being manic-depressive," I said, in a clinical tone I sometimes get when I'm talking about her. "And she took lithium for years. But she wanted to get off it. She said it was making her hair fall out. And making her forget things all the time, like her lines, which was freaking her out. Or maybe she was freaking out because she started not taking it. I'm not really sure."

I flashed on the last time I saw her alive. We were at the coffee shop at the Edison Hotel, a hangout for actors near Times Square. We were sharing a piece of cheesecake and guzzling coffee. She was in rehearsals for an Off Off Broadway play. It should've been a wonderful time for her. And up until that day, it was. She had the best part in the best production she'd been cast in since moving to New York. And she was in love with Gerold, the playwright. And they were having a very hot affair.

Gerold was British, and she had a whole fantasy going that she would move with him to London and be Marilyn Monroe to his Arthur Miller (but with a happier ending).

The only problem was, he had a wife back home and a baby too. Diana knew about them, but was able to believe they would be deleted from the picture. But then the wife arrived, with the child, a week before opening night.

"Suddenly he's acting like he doesn't know me."

"That's rough."

"If he thinks I'm going to keep my mouth shut—"

"You're going to tell his wife?"

"She should know the truth."

"Forget about the affair, Diana. This is a great part for you. They have reviewers coming. Don't blow this!"

"Forget about the affair?! You see, you have no idea, Jennifer, you just don't. I'm fighting for what I want, and I love Gerold."

"Then you're being stupid, because he's obviously a jerk."

"Because he's having an affair with me? Thanks a lot."

"That's not what I mean."

"You should see his wife. She's an idiot. And he's madly in love with me. And I'm not going to let him give in to her just because he's afraid."

"Fine. It's your funeral."

Two days later she called me in tears. The wife had been sitting in on a rehearsal, which made Diana tense. When the director criticized something Diana was doing, she blew up at him. When Gerold wouldn't back her up, she blurted out about the affair. The wife threw a fit, Diana threw an even bigger fit, and the director fired Diana.

"There will be other plays," I said, thinking that even if there were, she'd have some variation on the same problems all over again.

"None that are written by Gerold."

"He's not worth it."

"But I love him."

I wanted to get off the phone. We'd been on the phone for three hours already going in circles, and nothing I could say was making her feel better and I just wanted to get off the phone.

"You'll get over him, Diana, you know you will."

"No I won't. He wrote that part. That part was perfect for me. It **was** me. How could he let this happen?"

"I don't know. Look, why don't you get some sleep? It will be better in the morning."

"No it won't. It will never be better. You don't understand. Gerold means everything to me."

"I'm sorry. But I have to hang up now. Okay?"

"You don't care, do you."

"I do care. But I'm really tired, and I don't know what else to say . . ."

"Fine. Go. Sorry to keep you up."

I could hear the icy tone in her voice. I can still hear it inside my head. "Call me tomorrow," I said.

"Good night, Jennifer."

She didn't call me the next day. I tried her once from work, but got the machine. I was relieved she didn't answer. I didn't want to have to listen to her go on more about Gerold.

When I got home from work, I set up a nice dinner for myself on the table. A turkey sandwich (with very little mayonnaise) from my favorite deli on Ninth Avenue. A bag of potato chips. And a can of Diet Coke. I had a copy of that day's *Post* with a juicy story about Madonna on the cover, and I was just about to sit down to eat when the phone rang. I picked it up with dread, assuming it was Diana. Now I'd have to hear about Gerold and his wife, or tell her to call back later, which would annoy her.

It was my mother. She'd spoken to Diana the evening before, after she'd hung up with me.

"She was inconsolable," my mother said. "I told her to call me today, but I haven't heard from her. I want you to go down to her apartment."

"Now?"

"Right now. Take a cab."

I looked at my turkey sandwich. I couldn't eat it now. I put it in the refrigerator. I never would eat it. As a matter of fact, after that day, I wouldn't eat much of anything for weeks.

And now, here I was, sitting with Kelly, looking down at a plate of crumbs from a cake I couldn't eat. Kelly was silent. I looked up at her. She smiled with sympathy and waited for me to say more.

"She was pretty unhappy. But that wasn't exactly unusual. And two weeks before she died, she was high as a kite. So how do you know when this unhappiness is going to be . . . you know . . . *the* unhappiness."

Kelly looked at me with such compassion. "You couldn't know," she said.

Again the tears. The stupid tears. I wiped them away as quickly as I could.

"I'm surprised it still gets me so upset."

"Are you kidding? Four years ago is like yesterday. That's asking a lot of yourself to be over it already. Who could have that kind of perspective?"

I wondered. Was she saying that as a sideways—or not so

sideways—criticism of my play? Was that why she had only said it was "good" not "great" not "fantastic"? Because she didn't think I had perspective? I hated feeling so insecure. It shouldn't have been so important for me to know she liked it.

"I think I do have a lot of perspective on it," I said. "Just maybe not as much emotional distance as I would want."

"Yes, well, that's why the play is so passionate. Your feelings are there. It's powerful."

I stretched my mouth into a smile, acknowledging the compliment though it didn't really feel like one. "I guess it's ridiculous how insecure we can all be about our work."

"I'm not insecure about my work," she said, "I know I'm talented."

She didn't say it like she was bragging. She said it like she was saying the simple truth.

I went home feeling utterly exposed. I never should've told her about my sister. Now I felt naked. Naked and unattractive. I went home wishing I could be more like Kelly. So incredibly self-confident. So well equipped to take on the world. Why did I have to be me? I was boring. Repressed. Uncool. And now I'd written a play about my uncool, boring, repressed self. Why did I think anyone would be interested in anything I had to say? For that matter, why did I write when I hated hearing the sound of my own voice?! So my play must be a piece of garbage. Instead of sending it to Peter, I should've dragged the whole file to the trash icon on my computer and clicked on EMPTY. But I didn't, so now we were all wasting our time on my moronic, stupid, idiotic play.

I let myself into my apartment. My "very own apartment in New York City." My "glamorous" Hell's Kitchen dump. And I got out my dustbuster and vacuumed out all the dustballs from under my bed and every corner. And I thought about all the negative thoughts I brought down on myself, and wondered why I did that. Kelly certainly didn't say mean things like that to herself. She said nice, supportive, affirming things. When I was done vacuuming, I got in bed and burrowed down under the covers. I didn't feel very lucky to be me. But at least, I reminded myself, I wasn't dead.

Chapter
5

Kelly's talent was obvious to everyone in the production. She was great at bringing out the sexuality and the aggression that were part of Julia. She had no discomfort with those qualities, and no inhibitions.

She also could take the passages where Julia talks about her own pain and make them very powerful. This made me feel good, because I had some worry that I'd slanted the play from the younger sister's point of view and I wanted the audience to feel for both sisters and see both points of view.

Annie was having a little more trouble with her role. She was still having a hard time making Melanie a worthy opponent. She tended to be too passive. To let Julia win too easily. I worried the audience would just think she was a loser and wouldn't care about her.

I listened as they worked through the second scene of the play. A year has passed, and Melanie is engaged to be married. And unsure if she can go through with it.

Melanie: *"I'm just not sure what I want anymore."*

Julia: *"You can't get married for them. You have to put yourself first. You have to be selfish."*

Melanie: *"But all the planning . . . the expense . . ."*

Julia: *"You can't think about that!"*

Melanie: *"It would hurt George incredibly!"*

Julia: *"Wouldn't it be worse marrying him when that's not what you really want? Wouldn't that be hurting him much more?"*

Melanie: *"I just . . . I don't know. I don't want to hurt anyone."*

Melanie paused there and looked at Julia intently before continuing.

Melanie: *"Why does it feel like whatever I do, someone is going to get hurt?"*

Meaning Julia, I thought. I hoped Annie understood I meant Julia would get hurt.

Julia: *"If you want, I'll tell Mom and Dad. And Dad will tell George, and then Mom will call everyone, and it will be just like it was never going to happen."*

Melanie: *"But it's crazy."*

Julia: *"It's okay. If you need to be crazy . . . then be crazy."*

Melanie was silent there for a long moment.

Or she was supposed to be.

But Annie didn't take a moment at all.

"Okay," she said. Way too casually. She wasn't feeling it. I looked at Peter to see if he was picking up on this. But I knew to keep quiet. It was too early in rehearsal for me to say anything, probably too soon for him too. We had to give the actresses time to find their way.

Kelly, as Julia, went to stand right behind Melanie. She put her hand on her shoulder. Don't touch her, I wanted to say. They wouldn't touch now.

Or maybe they would. Maybe that was just me who wouldn't have touched. But my sister would've. Maybe Kelly's instincts were right. I kept quiet.

Julia: *"Are you sure? Because this has to be your decision."*

Again, Melanie should've taken her time there. But Annie responded too easily.

Melanie: *"Yes."*

Julia: *"Fine. I'll go tell Mom and Dad."*

Kelly walked to where the door would be.

Julia: *"I'm glad that I'm here to help. After all. That's what sisters are for. Right?"*

Annie suddenly stood up and broke character. "I'm having a big problem with this."

"Okay, let's talk about it," Peter said.

"I find it hard to say these lines. My impulse would be to murder this woman, but Melanie lets Julia walk all over her."

"Yeah, well that's your own head, Annie, you have to get inside Melanie's head."

"I'm trying. It's just . . . she's so weak."

Annie glanced slightly at me, and I tried not to flinch.

"But she's not weak," Peter said. "She's quite strong. But it's an inner strength."

"An inner strength? She let her sister talk her out of getting married!"

"Even that, she's doing out of strength."

"I'm sorry, but I don't see it that way."

"She's doing it for her sister. To protect her older sister, who would be devastated."

"Why? I mean, it's not like it actually would devastate her."

"Melanie thinks it would."

"But she's wrong!"

I had to keep my mouth shut. This was Peter's job, to talk to the actresses. It was a special skill that I knew I didn't have. Some writers can, or think they can, and they direct their own plays. But there's a whole art to putting things in a way that will help the actors and not just sound like criticism. Plus a director doesn't have to feel defensive about the writing.

And Annie's objections to this scene made me feel insecure. Maybe the younger sister was totally weak . . . and therefore unsympathetic . . . like me . . . and so the play must be totally flawed . . . like me . . . and in fact the older sister was the only one who the audience would care about.

I looked to Peter for his response, wishing he would say something here that would answer her brilliantly. Explain the play, explain my life. Kelly, too, who had been silent, looked at Peter and waited.

"It doesn't matter if she's right or she's wrong," he said. "That's not for us to be able to know. The important thing is that's how she feels."

Annie said nothing to that. She was unconvinced.

"Hold on to this frustration," he said. "And use it. Let it be there, beneath everything Melanie says. But you can't let it out yet. You have to hold it in until the last scene. Okay, let's go on."

I could see by the troubled look on her face that Annie was not satisfied. She didn't look at me as they went on. I wanted to tell her it was okay, I understood. I knew Melanie could be frustrating. Give her time, I wanted to tell her, because she would get better before the end.

After rehearsal was over Annie took off right away. I glanced at Kelly thinking wistfully of cake and coffee, but she didn't meet my glance, gathered her things, and left with a quick good-bye.

I wondered if this was a bad sign. A lack of enthusiasm for the project. Or maybe they just needed a little personal distance as they worked through finding their parts. Or maybe they just needed to get somewhere.

Oh well, I reminded myself, it's not like I should expect to get reassurance from everyone about my play after every single rehearsal. If I'd learned anything from my previous productions (and being around Diana) it was that actors were the ones who needed to be reassured. Writers get to do multiple rewrites before they show their work to anyone. Actors didn't have the chance to correct their mistakes before offering themselves up to the scrutiny of rehearsals.

So what happens when everyone needs to be stroked? Who is there to do the stroking? I looked for Peter. As director, he was the ultimate parental figure. Full of confidence and superior knowledge. I joined him and Carol. They were talking about transporting some lumber to the theater for building the flats. Once that was figured out, Carol asked if Peter and I wanted to go to Rosie O'Grady's for drinks. I would've gone if Peter had said yes, but he didn't, and I didn't want to go alone with Carol. "No thanks," I said, hoping she didn't notice my initial partial nod.

She left, and I turned to Peter.

"Maybe I shouldn't keep coming to rehearsals," I said.

"Why?"

"I just think maybe my presence isn't good for the actresses. If they have problems with their parts, maybe they can speak more freely if I'm not around."

"Annie didn't seem to have a problem with that, and I don't think Kelly will either when she feels the need . . ."

"That's nice of you to say, but—"

"I'm not being nice. I want you to be at rehearsals. And you shouldn't be afraid to speak up. We're lucky to have you here. If we're screwing up, you can let us know. Listen," he said, "do you want to go out for a drink?"

"Sure." I tried not to let him see how pleased I was. Especially since he'd dodged Carol so we could be alone. "But I have to be at work in an hour."

"What do you do?"

"Word processing."

"Ahhhh."

"At a law firm."

"Mmm."

"Really boring. But the pay isn't bad. And I get to listen to music on my headphones when I type."

"There you go."

"And when it's slow, I can work on my plays and they don't even care."

"Sounds like a great job."

"Well," I said, "it's good for now."

It wasn't until we were down at Rosie O'Grady's, and after I'd looked around making sure Carol wasn't sitting somewhere nursing a drink all by herself, that I couldn't help but ask him . . .

"Do you think there was some truth to what Annie was saying? That she should put up more of a fight in that scene?"

"Do you?"

My answer came fast enough. "I think she's not there yet. She's too inside the problem. She doesn't see what she lets Julia do. Or what she lets herself do, for that matter."

"That's what I think," he said. "Look. When you take a play apart—do one scene over and over like we're doing—it's natural for the actor to want to fit the whole play into that one scene."

"Yes." I agreed. That made sense.

"When she has a chance to run through the whole play, she'll be able to pace herself. Annie isn't very experienced so she's probably feeling insecure."

"On the other hand," I said, "Kelly seems totally sure of herself. And she takes direction well, don't you think?"

"We were lucky to find her."

"We really were."

There was an awkward pause. I was aware that I was championing Kelly to him again (as if she needed that) and aware of wanting him to approve of Kelly (but not too much).

"So what do you do for a money job?" I asked. I had no idea how he earned his living, or how he could finance this play for that matter.

"Me? Oh . . . I live off the money I make producing plays."

"Ha ha."

"Just kidding."

Must have a trust fund, I thought.

"The truth is," he got serious, "I'm living off some money I inherited when my mother died. When that runs out in the not so distant future, I'm not sure what I'm gonna do."

"Oh. Wow. Sorry about your mother."

"Yeah." He took a sip of beer.

"How did she die?"

"Lung cancer. And yes, she smoked."

"So . . . you inherited . . . Were your parents divorced?"

"My father is dead too."

"Oh."

"He killed himself when I was sixteen."

I breathed in sharply. Now I knew why he'd been drawn to my play.

"You were so young. That must've been hard."

"It's okay," he said. "He was a mean son-of-a-bitch."

I waited for him to say "just kidding." But he didn't.

"I think that makes it even harder," I said. "Because you have to deal with . . . you know . . . your feelings of hate."

"Yeah. Like the character in your play." Peter looked at me and then looked away.

I flinched, because I wanted to say I didn't hate my sister. But then I registered he was referring to Melanie, not me. But did Melanie hate her sister? Hate was such a . . . hateful feeling.

"And, like the character in your play," Peter said, "my last conversation with my father was an argument."

I almost corrected him. My last conversation with my sister had not been a fight. Not really. I'd lost patience with her, and she didn't like that, but it wasn't a fight.

But he was referring to Melanie.

"What was the fight with your father about?"

"Oh, it was stupid. Really stupid." His lips clamped shut, and I wasn't sure if he was going to tell me what stupid thing it was. "I'd borrowed one of his favorite ties for a production of a Noel Coward play we were doing in school. I was acting in it. *Private Lives.* Just a stupid high school production. Didn't ask him for it, just took it. And then we all went out to eat after a late rehearsal. I had this big pastrami sandwich. And mustard dripped out of it, onto the tie. And it stained the tie really bad. I showed it to him the next day. Offered to dry clean it and everything. He was pissed. Really pissed off. My mom said nothing would get that out. I guess it was an expensive tie. He yelled at me . . . *I don't want you borrowing my fucking clothes again!* That night he took the car out. Got drunk. Smashed into a concrete divider on the highway and that was it."

I was silent for a few moments. Then I said, "You don't think of it as an accident."

"If you drink as much as he drank that night . . . and you get into a car . . . and you're speeding like a maniac . . . it's suicide."

"Well, obviously the tie . . . and his death . . . they didn't have anything to do with each other."

"Of course not," Peter said, a bit too defensively I thought. "Who knows what was going on inside his head. I'm sure it had very little to do with me. But . . . when I read your play, I related to Melanie's guilt feelings. Irrational as it is, you can't help it."

"Yeah."

So that's what we were. Two guilty souls. That's what drew us together.

"They say," Peter said, taking a sip of beer, "people take responsibility because at least that makes them feel like they have some control over what happened . . . instead of feeling so out of control . . ." His voice trailed off.

"I know."

I'd read all the books too.

"I bet it was a long time before you ate another pastrami sandwich," I said.

"Or mustard. Not even on hot dogs. And I used to love that stuff."

"Yeah." I nodded, thinking of cheesecake.

"Ironic thing is," Peter said, "I inherited all his clothes."

Ironic thing is, I thought, I wrote the play. And got the production. And got to meet you.

"Not that I can bring myself to wear any of it," he added.

Not that anything will come of it, I thought.

My parents were never the same after my sister died. For instance my mother used to leave cheerful outgoing messages on her answering machine. Like *"Don't worry about tomorrow. In two days it will be yesterday.* (BEEP)" And she'd record a new one every few months. But the day after my sister died she put a message on the machine that said, in this lost, helpless kind of voice, "She's dead." Then, after a few weeks, she changed it. "Please leave a message after the tone." Emotionless. Flat. It had been four years, and she still hadn't changed that message.

My father, who had always struggled with depressions of his own, seemed more depressed. I tried to comfort myself with the thought that he always knew the world was a sad place and her death just confirmed what he already knew.

But my mother seemed more done in. The death put her in a new place. The world was no longer amusing. The world was downright cruel.

Nothing was ever the same for me either, of course. That day my mother called and told me to go down to Diana's apartment . . . I knew, even as I was going through it, that my life was changing before my very eyes. I was so tense I couldn't find the key to her place, which I always kept in my jewelry box. (I found it a month later right there in my jewelry box.) So I had to go without it, wondering how I was going to get in. My mother had said take a cab, and I was going to. But then for some reason I ended up in the subway. I wasn't sure why. I told myself it was faster. But I would still have to get across town by walking or taking a bus or getting in a cab after all, so it wasn't really. But my sister always rode the subway, so it seemed right. So the whole way down I was kicking myself for getting on the subway. When I got out on West 4th Street, I hailed a cab. And then I realized that maybe this was the fastest way after all, so why was I kicking myself? Maybe it was because I didn't really want to take the fastest way. Because I didn't want to find what I was going to find. Not that I thought that I was actually going to find what I was going to find.

I mean, for all we knew, my sister had reconciled with Gerold. And they were in some hotel room making love, and Diana just hadn't bothered to phone anyone to say that life was wonderful again. And here I'd ruined a perfectly good evening because my mother was freaking out.

When I got to her building and managed to get a neighbor to buzz me in, I knocked on her apartment door. No answer. I couldn't find the super, so I called a locksmith. He told me we couldn't get in without the police, so I had to call them too. While I waited for everyone to arrive, I called my parents collect on a pay phone down the street. "I'm waiting to get in," I said.

"We'll be right here," my mother said.

A half hour later no one had arrived yet. It was beginning to get dark. I went to the pay phone down the street.

"Yes?" my mother answered. I could hear the panic in her voice.

"I'm still waiting to get in. Just wanted to let you know."

I knew my father was on the other line, but he stayed silent.

"We're here," my mother said.

When I finally called home from my sister's phone (which she'd decorated with glitter nail polish and a picture of Kurt Cobain) they picked up after one ring. My father was on one extension, my mother on the other. The policeman was standing somewhere behind me. Even now, my stomach sours at the memory.

"I got into the apartment," I said.

And then I paused. Because how do you tell your parents such a thing?

"She's dead."

"What?" my father said to my mother. "What did she say?"

"She said she's dead," my mother said. As if she had known from the moment of my sister's last breath because she was so psychically connected, and I was just there to confirm her fears.

"Are you sure?" my father asked, desperate.

"Yes. The policeman is here."

"Put him on the phone," my mother said.

As if I wasn't telling the truth. As if I would be careless about getting my facts straight on this.

I put the policeman on. He repeated the news. And then he said he was sorry to them. And he said good-bye. And he hung up.

"Didn't they want to speak to me?" I asked.

He looked back at the phone, then at me. "You want to call them back? I'd like to keep the line open—I'm expecting backup." Backup. As if a crime was in progress and the sharpshooters were on their way.

"No, that's okay."

I told myself it was okay that my parents hung up. They were very upset right then. So they couldn't comfort their child. They had to comfort themselves, and each other. And they knew I was strong, and I could take care of myself. So I shouldn't take it personally that they hadn't said good-bye. They were in shock. And I would be fine.

I sank down into my sister's easy chair. The one she liked to read in. And I asked her how she could do this. How could she actually do this?

And I tried not to think of her face. The one I'd just seen. But I couldn't stop seeing it—her face was all I could see. Even in death, she seemed to be saying, "You think you have it bad? Don't flatter yourself. I'm the one who's suffering here. Look at me."

Chapter
6

It's always sort of a liberation for the actors to reach the point of having their lines memorized. A relief to put the scripts down and be able to walk around the stage with the words coming out of their mouths as if they were making them up that very moment. As if the lines were, in fact, their own thoughts.

This was also an exciting stage in rehearsals for me. My play would suddenly become much more real. Something much more apart from myself. And it would transform from being a script, words on the page, to being the physical "spoken out loud by real walking and talking human beings" thing that it was always meant to be.

Annie and Kelly had not reached that point yet. They were still chained down with the scripts, halfway between reading blocks of dialogue and remembering wisps of phrases. Since it was just the two of them in the play, they each had a lot of lines, and a lot of pressure.

I knew they were trying to get together from time to time to run lines, but their schedules didn't seem to mesh very well and it was getting frustrating for everyone that they weren't off book yet. It was Kelly who called me and asked if I would come over to her place to run lines.

"Annie was going to come, but she had to work, and I could use the help."

"Sure," I said. I thought it would be fun.

"I'll make you dinner," she offered.

"You don't have to do that."

"I insist. I love to have the chance to cook for someone."

"Well. Okay," I said. As if I needed to be enticed.

I was curious to see her place. Her life still seemed mysteriously full of unrevealed secrets. And I felt like, with the play and everything, she could piece together a lot about me, and that seemed like an unfair advantage. Especially because I'm someone who usually likes it the other way around. Kelly had managed to get around that. Unusual for an actress. They tend to blurt out everything that's bothering them. Maybe, I hoped, maybe tonight she'd be ready to blurt.

Kelly lived in the East Village a few blocks from where my sister used to live. It was just a coincidence, but it seemed like fate. I rarely went to that neighborhood, avoided going near her apartment. My last memories were too painful. Loading Diana's bed and dresser onto the Salvation Army truck. Taking her cat to a friend's apartment. Returning her books to the library. Closing her bank account.

As I walked down the familiar streets, I kept looking for her face in the crowd. My heart beat faster and I felt a twisting feeling in my stomach. Here was the hardware store where I'd helped her pick out a fan. Her favorite shop to buy used CDs. Veselka's, the Ukrainian coffee shop we used to go to for blintzes. We loved going there and ogling Max, one of the cooks, who didn't speak any English but had this beautiful surfer-boy blond hair.

I purposefully avoided going by her building. As if I would

find her there sitting on the stoop. It was odd enough that I was back in the neighborhood visiting the actress who would be playing her.

Kelly lived in a walk-up over a greasy Chinese takeout. I suppose there's a certain glamour to grunge. It wasn't like I lived in a palace myself. But I was pretty disappointed to see how dreary it was. I wanted something better for her. Of course, I told myself even then, eventually this apartment would just become a colorful detail in the story of her rise to fame and glory. I did read in *People* recently that she bought a house with a swimming pool in the Hollywood Hills.

She buzzed me in, and I walked up the creaky wooden steps. These buildings always had a certain smell to them. I don't know from what. Rusted pipes? Rat droppings? Sauerkraut? All of the above? There was a gigantic schmushed dead waterbug on the stairway.

On the second-floor landing, I passed a very pale man with a shaved head and a bulging belly that made him look about seven months pregnant. He just stood in the doorway to his apartment watching me. Large black dogs behind him barked like crazy.

Finally I reached her floor. She had her door propped open for me and I went on in. She was at a small stove stirring something in a pot and the apartment smelled cozy with tomato sauce.

"Come in! Dinner is almost ready."

Needless to say, she wasn't famous then, and she was in this crummy apartment, but I already felt totally flattered that she was cooking for me. As if someone famous was cooking for me, and why me, a total nobody. But the room, I saw as I came in, was depressing. She had a small studio somewhat like mine. But she'd done nothing to decorate it. There was nothing on the walls, no curtains. Just lots of books stacked in piles and on some shelves. It was as if she was camping out. Like she knew she wouldn't be there for long, so why bother. A loft bed was built into the dark end of the apartment, and a small round table and two chairs were by the two gated windows that looked out the back of the building.

"I hate this apartment," she said. "But it's cheap, and it's all mine. I don't think I could bear to live with someone else."

"Well, hopefully you won't have to live here for long."

"That's right. We'll get such great reviews from *Til Death Do Us Part*, it'll move to Broadway and the rest will be history."

"Yeah, well, I'll be happy if we get the reviewers to show up at all."

"They say it's better to get bad reviews than no reviews," she said.

That was a sentiment I couldn't really embrace.

"But you won't get a bad review," she added.

"Certainly **you** won't get a lousy review—that's unimaginable."

"Thank you, that's very sweet of you. So listen. I was hoping we could run the lines first because after I eat and have some wine I won't be able to concentrate. So if you're not hungry . . ."

"That's fine."

"Good. I'm going to stand, but if you want to sit here at the table, or stand, it's up to you."

I sat at the table and got out my script. "Where do you want to start?"

"I thought we'd just begin with the beginning."

"Whatever you want. This is for you."

So we started.

It was odd, reading my own lines out loud. I'd heard them a thousand times over in my head when I was writing, but I'd never spoken them out loud.

Julia: *"So how do you like your new apartment?"*

Melanie: *"It's small. No view. The ceiling is low. It never gets a drop of sun. And I've already stepped on two cockroaches. It's the epitome of Hell's Kitchen—"*

Julia: *"Glamour!"*

Melanie: *"I was going to say grunge. I never thought I'd feel lucky to live in a place with bars on the windows."*

I put down my script. "This is weird. To be saying these lines. I feel so awkward."

I was frustrating myself, because I was saying them very stiffly, and it made my own play sound stiff.

"Don't worry about it," she reassured me. "We don't need to get the meaning, just run the lines."

"I know, but when you say the lines they have meaning and when I say them they sound so awkward! You make it seem so effortless."

"You want to run them again?" she asked.

"Do you want to?"

"No, I just get the feeling *you* want to."

I laughed. "That would be silly!"

"Maybe it would feel good for you, to say them."

"I just . . . It's very strange. When I write it, I hear it exactly how I want it to sound. And here I'm trying to say it out loud. And I can't make it sound the way I want to."

"You're afraid of the words."

"The feelings behind the words."

"But it was your feelings that came up with the words."

"But I can't say them out loud."

"Well, it's true," she said. "A confrontation that's totally imagined is different from confronting someone in real life."

"But this isn't real life. I can't even pretend to confront."

"Try again."

We started from the beginning. I was better the second time. As we continued on, I managed to loosen up a little.

Julia: *"You really have to develop a thicker skin, Melanie, or people are just going to take advantage of you."*

Melanie: *"I know."*

Julia: *"And you have to think positively if you want to get anywhere in this world."*

Melanie: *"You're right. I know. Theoretically."*

This is the scene when Julia goes to the window, slides open the gate, raises the window and screams out. Kelly put down her script, went to her window, slid the gate open and raised the window. As she did, she continued with her lines. She seemed to know them all perfectly.

Julia: *"Now I want you to repeat after me."*

Kelly put her head out the window and screamed.

Julia: *"I am ambitious!"*

Melanie: *"No."*

Julia: *"Say it! Go ahead."*

She motioned to the window.

Melanie: *"This is idiotic."*

Julia: (yelling) *"I am ambitious!"*

Kelly looked at me expectantly.

I walked to the window.

Melanie: *"I am ambitious."* I said with no spirit.

Julia: (yelling) *"And I deserve to succeed!"*

Melanie: *"Do I have to?"*

Julia: (yelling) *"I deserve to succeed!"*

Melanie: *"I deserve to succeed. I suppose."*

Kelly broke from the script. "Let's do it again."

"But you know the lines."

"I want to do it again and I want you to really try screaming out the window."

She said it like she was a director and she was trying to adjust my performance. "But Melanie wouldn't scream." In real life Diana didn't even get me to the window.

"But I want you to scream."

I looked at her. I looked at the window. I could not imagine screaming so her actual neighbors, like that man below with the dogs, would hear.

Kelly jumped back into the script.

Julia: *"You have to think positively if you want to get anywhere in this world. Now I want you to repeat after me."*

She stuck her head out the window again and yelled.

Julia: *"I am ambitious!"*

I started to giggle. "No!"

"Go ahead!"

I tried, but it got mangled with more giggles.

Melanie: *"I am ambitious!"*

"Try again," Kelly said. "And mean it."

I forced myself not to laugh.

Melanie: *"And I deserve to succeed!"*

"Louder."

I screamed at the top of my lungs. *"And I deserve to succeed!"*

Kelly yelled after me. *"And I deserve to succeed!"*

We screamed it together, in unison, and that time I really yelled. *"And I deserve to succeed!"*

"Excellent!" Kelly said.

"I did it!"

"And God didn't strike you dead."

"Not yet, at least," I said, looking nervously up towards the sky.

"Anyway," she said, closing the window, "I have to get going."

She had to go? Where? "I thought we were going to have dinner."

"That's the line, silly."

"Oh. Right. Your acting is so natural." I felt embarrassed. I actually blushed.

Kelly laughed. "Are you hungry?"

"Sort of."

"So let's eat."

"Don't you want to finish the first act?"

"I'm hungry. And it smells so good."

It did smell good.

"We'll try to be good and do more after we eat."

"Well, okay, if you're sure."

"Come, sit down. I made your favorite," she said, going to stir the pot on the stove. "Spaghetti with sweet Italian sausage."

I bristled. "Very funny." This was a line from my play. When Julia cooks for Melanie.

"But I did. I hope you do like it."

"Well . . ." I was tempted to say I didn't. Just to prove that I made things up. But I really did like Italian sausage, and ultimately I didn't want to hurt her feelings. It truly seemed like she did it to please me. "I do. But I like a lot of other things too."

"Don't get all defensive," she said, "so you like Italian sausage and your sister killed herself. Two things in the play that are true to life."

She was smiling at the absurdity in it, but I didn't find it funny.

"You seem intent on ferreting out everything in the play that's based on something real. It's annoying."

"Hey, relax. Have some wine."

I sort of glared at her as she poured me some red wine.

"Sweetie," she said, "it doesn't matter to me how much of the play is real and how much you made up."

"Then stop trying to trap me."

"It's not a trap," she said, pouring herself wine.

"Then why do you get that look on your face, like you caught me?!"

"I don't! You're just imagining."

"No I'm not!"

"Would you chill out?"

I took a sip of wine. Drop it, drop it, I told myself. I didn't want to sit here and argue with her. But it was annoying. Tonight was the night I was supposed to finally find out about *her* secrets and it kept being all about mine. She sipped her wine and went to get the noodles out of the boiling water. The spaghetti sauce was making my mouth water.

"You're right," I said. "I'm being overly sensitive."

"Well I'm sorry if I stepped on your toes."

"It's okay. Forget it." I took another sip of wine. So did she.

"So," I said, "you work as a bartender?"

"Yeah."

"Where?"

"This bar called Wallpaper down in Soho."

"Must be interesting."

"You think so?"

"The guys must try to pick up on you all the time, right?"

"No."

"Really?"

"I don't know." She seemed annoyed. The same way it annoyed me when she was nailing down what was or was not made up in my play. "I suppose they would. If I let them. But I'm not standing around flirting like you think. It's hard work."

"Yes, but it must get slow sometimes, and then you're just standing there while some drunk slob is staring at you . . ."

"They can stare all they want."

"It doesn't creep you out?"

"You're the one who doesn't like people looking at you." She'd done it again. That was in the play.

"Sorry," she said. "I shouldn't make that assumption. Just because the character of Melanie doesn't like people to look at her doesn't mean that you—"

"I *don't* like people to look at me. So you found another

one," I said, taking another sip of wine. "By the end of the evening maybe we'll find out that every single line of that play, every detail, is totally and absolutely verbatim and unfictionalized."

Kelly put a mound of noodles on each of our plates and then ladled a generous amount of sauce on top.

"Just because it's about you," she said, "doesn't mean it hasn't been fictionalized."

"Right," I said hesitantly.

"As long as the writer has the perspective on herself, or whoever, to see the story. The beginning, the middle and the end. And the end has meaning. It's not just 'the way it happened.' Then it's fiction. Not just therapy or indulgence."

"And do you think my play has a beginning, middle and an end?"

"I believe in your play. Otherwise I wouldn't be doing it."

I noticed the evasion. "Maybe you just see a good part for yourself."

"Why are you doing this? It isn't my place to decide if your play is good or not. I'm just the actress."

There was some truth to this. She was just the actress, and I shouldn't have cared so much. "I don't know why," I said, "but it seems like I want your approval."

"Well, you already have it, so relax."

I took another sip of wine. It was going to my head.

"I hope I'm not going to be too drunk to run lines with you."

"Don't worry," she smiled, "I'm sure you'll do fine."

"You're the one who has to memorize them, thank god. I don't know how you do it."

"I'm a quick study. And once you have the lines, that's when it starts getting fun. That's why I like to get them down quickly. It holds you back when you're dependent on the script."

"If I thought, while I wrote them, about the fact that some-one would have to memorize all those lines . . . I don't think I would feel right having them say so much! I mean if you think about it, the effort that goes into putting on a play is so out of proportion to the payoff."

"Do you believe that?"

"Well. Not if it becomes a classic and it's done all the time all over the world. But if it takes the usual route of a small production that comes and goes and no one ever sees it . . . This spaghetti is so good, by the way."

"I'm glad you like it."

We both ate in silence.

"I'm sorry if I sound like I complain a lot. About the the-ater."

"I don't care. Complain away."

"We all know how hard it is."

"And we do it anyway."

"I was wondering about you, though . . ."

"Yes. . . ?"

What I really wanted to know was if she had a boyfriend, or since it didn't seem like she did, what her last serious relation-ship was. "You went to Juilliard?"

"Uh huh."

"Were people there good?"

"The people were great. I had classes taught by some amaz-ing people. Kevin Kline. Judi Dench. It was a great program."

"That's great." I took another bite. I waited to see if she'd say more. She didn't.

"Did you stay in touch with any of those people? The other students?"

"Some of them."

"It's good to have a network of people. You can help each other out."

"Sometimes."

I felt determined that I was going to get her to talk about herself, but she seemed equally determined not to reveal anything.

Then she paused in her eating and smiled at me with this little mischievous look.

"So what's the deal with you and Peter?"

"Peter?"

I felt flustered.

"Are you sleeping with each other?"

"What?"

"You heard me."

And suddenly I found myself once again struggling with how much I was going to tell her about myself.

"There is nothing going on with me and Peter."

"I don't believe you."

"I hardly even know him."

"You two seem very close to me."

"We just met a few months ago. I sent my play to his theater. He liked it. We met. He offered to do this production . . ."

"And here I thought you two were an item from way back, and you were just playing it cool in front of us."

"No. It's not like that at all."

"So . . . there's nothing going on between you two? You're not attracted to him?"

I was about to answer her, and then, in the nick of time, I turned it around. "Are you attracted to him?"

And for this question, I got a payoff. She smiled with pleasure. "Well. I think he is adorable."

"You do?"

"Oh, yes. I would love to get him in my bed."

It was annoying. Why did she have to like him of all people in the universe? "So are you going to make a move on him?"

"I don't see why not. Especially if you have no claims."

Did I have a claim? I thought of the kiss on my cheek. That

was sort of a claim. But the idea of declaring him for myself when she wanted him made me feel anxious. It was important to keep her happy for the production. That was the most important thing. I needed her to stay happy.

Now I suspected more than ever that he was her main reason for deciding to do my play. Maybe even my presence here in her apartment wasn't to read lines at all, but was to clue her in about Peter. The dinner and the wine and the compliments were all, in the end, about finding a way to him.

Though that didn't make sense. She didn't need to get to him through me. If she wanted him, I had no doubt, she could get him. Walk right over me.

In any case, I really couldn't fathom the idea of competing with her. After all, she had sex as a weapon. I was basically unarmed.

"I like him. And he likes me," I said. "But that's all there is to it."

The next week I had to miss a couple rehearsals because they had a rush of work at my job and called me in for extra hours. I rationalized that, despite what Peter had said, it was just as well to let the actors work without me staring down their throats. But it seemed so contrary to the point of my whole existence to be in a law office sitting in front of a computer typing up cover sheets for co-op conversions when I knew that in a small mirrored room on 27th Street two actresses, a director and a stage manager were all focusing their attention on my play.

I tried to comfort myself with the thought that if I was a successful playwright, my plays would be done all over the world, and I could never hope to be at all the productions—not even for opening night, much less rehearsals. But my plays weren't being done all around the world. And I was lucky it was being done at all. I put on my headphones and dug out an

old favorite—Sheryl Crow being passionately depressed—and
made myself forget about the party I was missing.

I returned to rehearsal on a Thursday evening. I couldn't
help but wonder if Kelly had made a move on Peter yet, but it
didn't seem like it. As everyone straggled in, I noticed the
mood was not exactly cheery. Peter looked worried. Annie
looked distressed. Kelly looked grouchy. Nobody seemed par-
ticularly happy to see me. Or happy to be there. Or happy to
be doing what they loved most in the world.

The honeymoon was definitely over.

At this point, what was uppermost on everyone's mind was
that they were putting in an awful lot of time and hard work
and not getting paid. Certainly the actresses were wondering,
"Who is this know-it-all director pestering me about lines
when he's lucky I showed up at all today? And why aren't I
working on Broadway like so-and-so who has half as much talent as I do?!"

They were trying to do the third scene of the play off book.
But they couldn't go more than a few lines without messing
up.

Julia: *"And so, my dear sister, I know this would be terribly inconvenient for you, and you like your privacy and everything, but I need
to ask if I can move in with you."*

Melanie: *"Here?"*

Julia: *"Just until I find something else."*

Melanie: *"But what about your cat?"*

Carol interrupting. "The line is: 'But it's so small! And what
about your cat!'"

Melanie: *"But it's so small! And what about your cat!"*

Julia: *"You'll love living with kitty. You know how she loves her
Aunt Melanie."*

Adores her Aunt Melanie, I thought, the word is *adore*, not
loves. Carol didn't correct her. Did she think it was too small a

correction to stop them? She'd just made a small correction, maybe she didn't want to make another one. Or did she just not notice. Or maybe she preferred the word "loves." Would Kelly catch it later? Should I tell her? Was it worth the bother?

Melanie: *"But there's nowhere for you to sleep."*

Julia: *"I'll sleep on the floor. Can you imagine an easier house-guest?"*

Melanie: *"There must be someone. One of your friends . . . with a bigger place. What about Jeffrey?"*

Julia: *"What about his wife?"*

Melanie: *"I thought he was divorcing her."*

Carol: "'I thought he was really getting ready to divorce her.'"

Melanie: *"I thought he was really getting ready to divorce her."*

"Line?" It was Kelly. Carol read out her line.

"'He is. He hates her. And he's madly—'"

Julia: *"He is. He hates her. And he's madly in love with me. But he's afraid, you know. It's complicated."*

"Line?" This time it was Melanie.

Carol: "'But did you talk about it in a direct—'"

Melanie: *"But did you talk about it in a direct way?"*

Julia: *"Yes! That's why we're fighting! He doesn't want to!"*

"I'm sorry," Annie interrupted. "I'm sorry, but I have trouble with this."

Kelly put her script down with impatience.

"Why," Annie complained, "doesn't she let her sister move in with her? I mean Julia is losing her own apartment, she's broke, her boyfriend is screwing her, she's lost her job. How can Melanie be so heartless?"

But don't you see, I'm thinking, this is good that she's finally saying no. She's not letting herself be bullied. You've been complaining about Melanie being too passive so enjoy the fact that she's finally standing up for herself!

"I'm glad that you're seeing it that way, Annie," Peter said.

"Because that's just how Melanie sees it too. She's finally saying no, but it's tearing her apart inside because she feels like she should be saying yes. She always feels it from Julia's point of view. So this is very hard for her. So don't let go of all those conflicted feelings, even while you speak the words that Jennifer has written."

"I don't know," Annie said. "It doesn't feel right."

She avoided looking at me.

They continued. Doggedly. Stumbling over the lines.

"Can we take that again?" Kelly asked.

"I don't know what's wrong with me today," Annie said.

"Line?" Kelly said, missing another line.

"Line?" It was Annie's turn. "Fuck me," she said, "fuck me," as if to ward off Peter's criticism. "Fuck me!"

"Ladies!" Peter finally blew up. "You have to learn your lines! We open in two weeks! How do you expect to rehearse if you don't know the fucking lines?!"

We were now, I felt, clearly at that point in rehearsal where everyone, collectively, without having to say it out loud, hated the play.

Any doubts or insecurities they had about it to begin with (previously put on the back burner because of course you want to give the benefit of the doubt to this project you've been chosen to be involved in) were now in full flower. The play was horribly flawed. Bound to flop and embarrass us all.

I sat in the back row, mortified and guilt stricken. I was sorry that I had written the play at all and compelled them into performing it. Because, let's face it, this wasn't really a play. It was a sadistic exercise to force unsuspecting people into experiencing a re-creation of some of the worst moments of my life.

And now the play was ruling their lives like a crazed dictator, holding them captive in its insane little world.

Peter called a break. Everyone separated off. Annie sat in

one corner whispering her part to herself. Carol took out a sandwich and started to eat. Peter went out in the hall and Kelly followed him. I stifled the urge to go to each and every one of them and apologize profusely for having inflicted this nightmare onto them.

Of course, none of them were prisoners. And I was fully aware that they could walk out and never come back any time they wanted. And there would be nothing I could do about it.

I wondered what Peter and Kelly were doing out in the hall. Maybe she had already made a move on him. And they were doing a good job of hiding it from the rest of us. And right now they were together in the bathroom, making out. Because they just couldn't stand having to keep their hands off each other during these tedious rehearsals.

Annie looked up from her script. Our eyes met. I wanted her to know that I wasn't mad that she didn't like Melanie (and by extension me) because I could understand how frustrating this character could be. So I offered to get her some tea or coffee from the deli down the block.

"No, thanks, I have water."

She picked up the ubiquitous plastic bottle of water that all actresses carry with them like birth control and took a sip.

"Are you sure," I asked. "Are you hungry? Because I could pick you up something to eat. A sandwich . . ."

"No, I'm fine, really."

I looked towards the door, hesitating. I didn't want to find Peter and Kelly out there in a passionate embrace. Safer to stay here.

Annie saw the worry on my face.

"I'm sorry," she said. "I don't want you to feel like I don't . . . I love this play. And even though I'm struggling here, you know, this is just my way. This is how I work. And I have to work through it. So don't be freaked out if it seems like I'm having a hard time. Okay?"

"Okay," I said. "Thanks."

We smiled. It felt good to be reassured. It didn't sound like she was going to quit. She might ruin the play, but she wasn't going to quit.

With that settled, curiosity overtook me. I ventured out into the hallway.

Kelly was sitting on the floor mouthing her lines. Her lines, my lines, just an annoyance to her now, an obstacle to overcome so that she could get out there and show the world what a great actress she was.

Peter was on his cell phone with some business to take care of. It seemed like he had endless demands. The postcards had to be sent out, the publicist pushed, the papers notified, critics invited, producers wooed. Producers with money, or money contacts. That was the key. A real producer could move the show to a bigger space with a longer run and real salaries and real advertising. And then the critics really would come. And then it would really have a chance.

"So, did you hear?" It was Carol, in a hushed voice, emerging from the theater, her sandwich consumed.

"What?"

"Come." She motioned me to the bathroom. Her voice was foreboding, and I prepared myself for bad news as I followed her through the door.

"Hear what?"

"Kelly cancelled Monday's rehearsal."

"Because?"

"She has an audition for some new series on HBO."

"Oh. Good for her."

"Yeah, if she gets it, they start filming immediately. That means she's gone, sayonara."

My stomach lurched. Of course she would get it. Why shouldn't she? Sure the competition must be incredible. But if it would ruin my play, then she would get the part.

"Does Peter know?"

"Oh, he knows. Haven't you noticed a little tension around here today?"

"Yeah, I just figured they'd all decided they hated my play."

"They don't hate your play. They may hate you for writing the play, but they don't hate the play . . ."

"Thank you."

"But seriously. If we lose Kelly, we'll just have to find someone else."

"Do you think we can?"

"We'll have to. We're lucky it's not a week later."

"By the time she knows if she has the part, it will be a week later. And remember how hard it was to cast that part in the first place."

"This is what happens when you can't afford an understudy."

"We'll just have to hope she doesn't get it," I said and we exited the bathroom.

Kelly was still sitting on the floor mouthing her lines. She looked up at us and smiled. And we smiled back.

I saw Peter was done with his call so I went to say hello.

"Hi," I said.

"How's it goin'?" he asked.

I felt confused by his question. Did he mean the rehearsal, which he could see was going lousy. Or did he mean my life, and the fact that we hadn't spoken in days.

At that moment, Kelly stood up and went back into the theater. We watched her silently. She gave me the slightest of raised eyebrows.

"Carol told me about Kelly's audition," I said to Peter as soon as she'd closed the door behind her.

"It's a bummer."

"You think we'll be able to replace her?"

I could see my nervousness annoy him.

"I don't know. I have enough to worry about."

"Right." I decided I should give him some distance. The last thing he needed was to deal with my free-floating anxieties.

We started back in, but he put his hand on my shoulder to slow me down. I turned to face him.

"Listen," he said, "if I seem sort of distracted . . . it's because I'm really overwhelmed right now. A lot of details to take care of. But you know it's all for your play, right?"

"Yes. I know."

I sat through the rest of rehearsal in a state of giddy anxiety. He did seem to like me. But he needed his space. But Kelly was going to make a move on him. What if he succumbed to her? How would I handle that? I couldn't exactly blame him for choosing her over me. After all, I would choose to **be** her instead of me. It was all I could think about during the rest of rehearsal. Who would leave with who.

"Okay, let's call it a day," Peter said with some relief when they reached the end of the scene. "Tuesday at three o'clock. Be sure to get some rest over the weekend. And learn your lines!"

I braced myself to see her leave rehearsal with him. To link arms, head to the elevator, get a drink at Rosie O'Grady's, be unable to refrain from kissing over their beers (tentatively at first, but then with more passion, forgetting to care what the other patrons thought) and then rush back to his place barely able to keep their hands off each other a minute longer before jumping into the sack.

Annie rushed off as usual, and Carol said her good-byes as I busied myself with putting my copy of the script into my bag and checking inside my purse for, well, nothing at all, in case Peter might want to come over to speak to me. But he was back on his cell phone. It was Kelly who came up to me.

"Are you heading out?" she asked.

I tried not to look towards Peter to see if he was looking at us. It was his last chance to say anything to me before the weekend. I wouldn't see him until Tuesday. That seemed so far away!

"Yeah," I said, and we walked out together, saying our good-byes together. Peter barely interrupted his phone conversation as he nodded and waved.

"So," I said to Kelly, as we walked to the subway, "Anything happening with you and Peter yet?"

"I asked him to a movie Saturday night."

My heart sank. "What are you going to see?"

"He said no. He told me he was busy."

"Oh, that's too bad." (Yea! My heart suddenly lifted, life was beautiful, there were cherry blossoms on every tree . . .) "Busy doing what?"

"Didn't say."

"Huh. Maybe he has a girlfriend we don't even know about."

"I don't think so."

"Hmmm. Well," I said, giving her advice I would never take myself, "maybe you should ask him out for Sunday. Just because he couldn't go Saturday doesn't mean you should take it as a personal rejection. Maybe he was legitimately busy."

"I did ask him for Sunday."

"Oh."

"He said he was busy then too."

"Oh. Well, he's very pressured, I guess. He needs the weekend to chill out."

I was saying that to myself as well as to her.

"If you ask me," Kelly said, "Peter worries too much. He needs someone like me to show him how to have a good time."

"Uh huh. Well," I said, as we paused at the stairs to the subway, "it's certainly not me he's having a good time with Saturday and Sunday night."

"Then how'd you like to go to a movie with me?"

"You mean like a date? Second best?" I teased, "cuz you couldn't get him?"

"No reason for both of us to sit at home."

"I have to say, I'm sort of shocked you don't have twenty thousand guys dying to go out with you."

"There are guys I could go out with. I just can't stand them."

"Okay. Then you must have eight trillion friends. Actresses. Models. Heiresses. People you go club hopping with . . ."

"I don't like club hopping," she said. "And other women don't like me. My beauty always seems to intimidate them."

"Well, okay," I said, pushing away the smallest hesitation that I would spend the whole evening watching all the men drool over her and ignore me. It wasn't a big deal. I was used to it. That's how it always was with my sister.

I slept in late the following morning and was woken up by the ringing of the phone. The machine picked up. It was Peter.

"Hi. Sorry I missed you," he was saying into the machine.

I looked at the clock. Eleven. I was undecided whether to eavesdrop on the message or speak to him.

"Give me a call," he was saying, "when you—"

I decided to pick up. "Hello?" Better to talk to him now than have the anxiety over calling him later.

"Hi. Did I wake you?"

"No!" Guilty, like I'd been caught masturbating (as if). "No, I wasn't sleeping, I was just getting some breakfast."

"Listen, I was wondering if you'd like to get together later."

"Tonight?" Damn!

"Yeah."

"Oh . . . you know . . . I can't."

"Oh. Well. It's my fault. I shouldn't have waited so long to ask. I was feeling so hassled yesterday I couldn't think ahead."

"Yeah. Well, things are in that chaotic sort of up-in-the-air stage . . ."

"I hope you aren't too worried."

"No . . ."

"Because I'm sure everything is going to work out."

I wished he were talking about us and not the play.

"I'm sure they will."

I told myself to ask him out for Sunday. Like I told Kelly to.

"You have to remember," Peter was saying, "it's tempting for an actress to want to see the character she's playing as being just like she is."

"Yes." Don't be afraid, I told myself. He had already told Kelly he was busy, but he was lying, right? Because he wanted to go out with me and not her, right?

"All she has to do," Peter was saying, "is insert herself in, and then everything comes easy. But if she has to imagine a personality that's different from her own, it's gonna take a lot more work . . ."

"You know, I am free on Sunday. If you want to do something on Sunday."

"Sunday is good," he said. "Around six?"

One, two, three, four, five . . . "Six is good."

"Great. So I'll pick you up at your place. We'll get some dinner."

"Great." I hate the way I sound when I say "great." It always sounds fake even though I don't mean it to be. And I certainly meant it then. Even though it sounded fake. "See you then."

Chapter
7

I wish I could skip the next part. Describing the night out with Kelly. Describing the night out with Peter. It's too much. I don't want to think about any of it. But I guess I should make myself continue. Maybe if I get a piece of chocolate I could bribe myself. Some chocolate with tea. That's what I'll do. If I get to have the chocolate and tea, I can make myself go on.

So. We met at the Waverly movie theater on Sixth Avenue. (I'm back with some tea and chocolate-covered raisins.) We saw a Brad Pitt movie. I don't go for Brad Pitt but she did. Little did we know she'd be in a movie with Brad Pitt in the not-so-distant future. Weird to think. But I guess, as we sat in that movie theater, she must've been imagining that for herself. Probably why she sighed on the way out. With that frustration of "Why can't it be me up there?" Though she didn't say it. It wasn't like Kelly to complain in that way. Lots of actresses complain all the time about how hard it is, but Kelly didn't.

"Are you hungry?" she asked.

"I could eat," I said. I wasn't really hungry but I didn't want to go home.

"Any ideas where we should go? There's a ton of restaurants around here."

"I don't know one from another."

"There's an Italian restaurant near my place. They have this fettuccine dish that I adore."

An actress who eats fettuccine. Amazing.

"But," she added, "it would take you out of your way."

This was true. Heading over to the East Side would mean a two-leg journey home instead of a quick straight-up on the subway.

"Maybe we should walk around a little," she said, seeing my hesitation. "We're bound to find something."

"That's okay. If you know they have good food at the place near you . . ."

"They have great food."

"Then maybe we should just go there. I can always take a cab home," I said, wondering why I was offering to inconvenience myself. I mean it was Manhattan. There are twenty restaurants on every block.

"Okay, let's go there." She seemed pleased. "The pasta is out of this world."

As we walked down the street, men kept turning to look. She did like revealing clothes. That evening she wore a tight red halter top, and she had a lot of cleavage spilling out. So she got constant comments. "Hey, mama, you hot. Look at those boobies. Come home with me, mama, I'll show you a good time . . ."

We had to ignore quite a few of these on this particular Saturday night. I suppose it bothered her, but I suppose it pleased her too. She certainly wasn't going to keep her body a big secret because of it.

The restaurant was dark and noisy, but we got a table in the back corner that gave us some privacy. Again, all the men's heads turning to look at her. Women too, for that matter. I felt tickled to be the one with her. Like it gave me some sort of status. Even though no one looked at me for a second, except maybe to be curious to see who was with her and then be disappointed when they saw it was just me.

Tonight, I thought, tonight I'm gonna get her to talk about her past, her family, her love life . . . I felt sure that after a glass of red wine and a big bowl of pasta she'd be ready to spill her heart out to me.

"So," Kelly asked me after the waiter took our order, "how do you feel about the way rehearsals are going?"

"Well. I know that Annie is struggling with her part. But I'm sure she'll find her way."

"She'll get there."

"I'm surprised she doesn't seem to like the part more," I added. After all—and this I did not say—Annie really had the lead. Julia wasn't the main character. She was the antagonist. It was a great role, but the play was clearly about Melanie. "Though I guess," and this I did say, "it's more fun to play a character like Julia who has the whole obnoxious, aggressive sexy thing going. No one likes to play the boring good character."

"I don't think of Julia as obnoxious."

"I didn't mean obnoxious, exactly. I certainly hope that I've made her understandable and sympathetic. Even though we don't always like her, we feel for her, and she's a lot of fun to be with, too, when she's not being difficult."

"I think she's complex. And intriguing."

"That's good."

"And I don't think Annie thinks of Melanie as boring and good. And I don't know where you get the idea that Melanie isn't sexy. I just think Annie is having a hard time getting under her skin. Sometimes it's hard to know what Melanie is thinking."

"Well, I think you're speaking from Julia's point of view," I said, wondering if she really did think Melanie was sexy. "Julia doesn't understand Melanie and what she's all about. But I think it's there, in the play, and Annie has to figure it out. Maybe it's found more in the subtext than in what she actually says."

I looked at Kelly, but she didn't seem convinced. "The play is very psychologically sophisticated," I said, my defensiveness rising. "It's not simple."

"No, it's not simple. And that's why it's so interesting. There are so many layers."

"Yes."

"It's just hard to get under all those layers."

"Well, that's the actor's job, right?"

"It's all of our jobs."

"You mean you don't think I did my job?"

"That's not what I said."

I was about to press her more, but the waiter arrived with our huge plates of pasta, and after that, through dinner, we avoided talking about anything having to do with the play. I realized that she still hadn't mentioned her audition. And neither had I. And it would be strange to do so now—maybe she thought so too—so it didn't come up. Peter didn't come up either. Nothing of any importance came up. And I felt like precious time was being wasted, talking about tired old subjects like expensive Manhattan real estate and the difficulty of finding a good person to cut your hair. I didn't want to bother with these mundane subjects, not with Kelly.

After the waiter cleared our plates away she sat back in her chair with a groan. "I am so stuffed."

"Me too. I should walk home. That would burn some calories at least."

"Are you going to?"

"No. Because if I walk, I won't get to bed for an hour and I'm exhausted."

Now I was regretting having walked over to her side of town for the restaurant. Especially since the conversation had been so disappointing. "I guess I'll blow ten dollars on a cab."

We split the bill and walked out to the street. The weather had turned nasty and it was starting to rain. I stood on the corner and tried to hail a cab as gusts of wind blew into my face.

But nothing came. Not a single empty cab.

"Maybe we should walk over to Second Avenue," I said. "It's on the way to your place and I should be able to find something there."

"Let's go."

When we reached Second Avenue I held my hand up. The rain came down harder. Still, no cab came by. "This is so weird," I said. "On a Saturday night."

It was starting to pour and neither of us even had coats.

"Look, why don't you come up to my place for a minute until this rain calms down. I'll make you a cup of coffee."

It was true she was right down the block. But all I wanted was to be at home in my nice warm bed.

"Well . . ." We stood there getting rained on. I looked once more up the street. Not only were there no cabs, but there were at least two other groups of people up the street also trying to hail cabs. I could've taken the bus to the subway, but the idea of getting on a train at this time of night was creepy and it would take forever to get home. My apartment felt like it was on the other side of the world. "Okay," I said. "I guess a cup of coffee sounds good."

So we went up the block to her building. The Chinese

take-out place was open and a few really depressed looking people were shoveling rice and noodles into their faces. She pushed open the heavy front door and we went up the stairs past the schmushed dead waterbug into her dreary little apartment.

She made me a very strong cup of coffee and we listened to the thunder outside.

"These summer rains can be amazing," I said.

"I like them," she said. "At least, when I'm all warm and cozy inside my own little apartment."

"Yeah," I said, thinking about the journey home I still had to take.

"Listen, why don't you stay here tonight?"

"You mean, like a sleepover? Like I used to have with my best friend Peggy Batshaw all the time?"

"Yes, we'll have our own little slumber party."

"But where would I sleep?"

I looked around. There was no couch or anything. Just the loft bed.

"In my bed."

"Your bed?"

I was slightly freaked at the idea of sharing a bed with her.

"Thanks, but I think I'll go home."

"Are you sure?"

"Yeah."

"It's not a big deal. I wouldn't mind at all."

"No. I'd rather go home. But thanks."

So I finished my coffee. And I said my good nights. And we kissed cheeks. And I tried not to notice how soft her cheek was. And she walked me to the door. "If you change your mind, come on back," she said.

"Okay, thanks," I said, and I went back down the stairs past the schmushed dead waterbug and out onto the street.

It was nasty outside. Bucketfuls of rain. Past midnight. And still no cabs!

I turned around and went back to her place and rang her bell.

Her voice came out of the intercom. "Hello!"

"I'm back!"

"Come on up!"

And she buzzed me in.

It was odd lying in bed next to her. I was very tense. I just could not relax. It's not like we were touching or anything. I just could not relax. It was like two in the morning, and I had dozed off for about an hour out of pure exhaustion and relief at being in a warm dry place, but then I'd woken up again, and my mind was racing. Racing with worry over the play, mostly. Kelly must've sensed that I was awake because she whispered to me, "Can't sleep either?"

I whispered too, as if there were someone else there who we shouldn't disturb. "I was asleep, but then I woke up, and now I can't go back."

"I can't sleep either," she said.

"Why not?" I wondered if she was excited about her audition for HBO.

"I was thinking about Peter," she began. "Trying to figure out why I'm so attracted to him."

Another thing I hadn't told her. That he'd asked me out. That we were seeing each other the next day. Which was already that day.

"So what do you think it is?"

"Probably just the old actress-director thing. They become so parental, it's like you can't help but want them to love you best."

"You mean like more than Annie?"

"Or you."

"Or Carol." We both sort of laughed at that.

"She gets to be with him more than any of us."

"I think she's madly in love with him," I said.

"I think so too."

And that's when I thought I might tell Kelly. Something about myself. Something that was a very closely guarded secret. Because I didn't want her to think that she had any reason to worry about competition from me. She should know that she had nothing to worry about. That any potential relationship I might have with Peter was doomed to fizzle as soon as he got closer to me. As soon as sex would enter the picture.

But I hesitated.

It was one of those horrible secret things that you never want anyone to know about yourself because it's so humiliating.

One of those horrible things that you want *everyone* to know. Because if they knew and they still thought you were interesting, then maybe it wasn't that bad.

And maybe they could even save you. From yourself.

"I have a confession to make," I said, looking into the darkness of the room.

"What?"

"Promise you won't lose all respect for me?"

"No."

"Then I can't tell you."

"Fine."

Silence. I couldn't believe she would leave it at that.

"Don't you want to know?" I asked.

"If you want to tell me."

"I don't want to tell you."

"Then don't."

Silence.

"I can't believe," I said, "that you aren't curious enough to hear what I might say that you won't reassure me that you won't judge me."

"But I probably will judge you. I won't be able to help myself."

"So lie."

"I don't want to lie."

"Lying to make someone feel reassured can be a good thing. Because it enables them to open up about something they're scared about, and then they'll probably be relieved once they're gotten it off their chest."

"Exposing yourself can be very upsetting. I'd think twice if I were you."

After a moment I said, "You don't tell very much about yourself, do you."

"I do when I want to."

"Because people can be cruel?"

"Because it isn't anyone's business."

"But . . ." I had to think about this. "Don't you think it's important for people to know about each other?"

"What do you mean?"

"To know the truth."

"What is the truth?"

"What do you mean?"

"There is no such thing as the truth," she said. "There's just what you want to believe."

Silence. Darkness. I could not sleep. The man with the pot belly and the dogs couldn't either, because we heard him taking them out on a walk. Evidently the rain had stopped.

"Maybe I should just go home," I said.

"Maybe you should just tell me," she said.

"But you just talked me out of it."

"But you want to."

"Can I trust you?"

"Probably not."

Having her tell me I couldn't trust her made me trust her more. So I forced it out of myself.

"I've never had an orgasm," I said.

"What?"

"You heard me."

Pause. Beat. Dizzy sensation.

"How old are you?"

"Twenty-five."

She didn't say anything for a few moments. And then she said, "That's sad."

"Pitiful. Right?"

"I had my first orgasm when I was seven."

"That's young."

"Yes."

"And you remember that?"

"Yes."

"So, what, someone . . . it was, like, incest or something?"

"No, silly. I gave it to myself. I was masturbating."

"Oh."

"Don't tell me you don't masturbate."

"Well . . ."

"You have to," she said, "or you'll never learn what you like. I mean, what do you do when you're in the mood and no one else is around?"

"I've tried. But . . ." I decided not to go into it.

"Wow," she said. "That's sad."

"The unpleasant facts about me are piling up, aren't they."

"We're going to have to do something about this."

I wasn't sure what she meant, exactly. Was she talking about a book? Some kind of instructional video? Hands on training? And was she referring to the orgasm problem or the masturbating or a package deal? I didn't know and didn't want to ask. I just felt relieved that someone finally knew who might actually be able to help.

"You know about your clitoris, right?"

"Yes. Of course."

"Don't you ever touch yourself there?"

"No."

"You're afraid to?"

"I just don't feel compelled to."

"Don't you think that's odd?"

"I don't know. I guess it is odd, yes, in this day and age it is very odd."

"So you have to do something about it. You have to explore. Touch yourself."

I have to say, I'm thinking this is a big mistake. I shouldn't be going into all this. It must make me seem like I was an idiot. People only want to hear about promiscuous women who have superficial one-night stands with men they meet at hip parties. Or famous movie stars. Not a depressed, boring, nonorgasmic younger sister. But I've gotten this far, so I guess I'd better go on.

"Once you learn how to bring yourself to orgasm," she said, "then you'll be able to tell your lover how to give you one."

This seemed utterly impossible to accomplish. It would be like wanting to be a cheerleader even though you'd never been able to do the splits. And then trying out for the squad and somehow managing, miraculously, to end your routine with the splits.

"If sex is such a natural thing," I said, "why does it seem so hard to get it right?"

"It is natural. If it doesn't get all screwed up."

"Well doesn't it seem like most people are screwed up one way or another?"

"I don't know about most people. A lot of people are, though." She paused and then she said, "I'm pretty screwed up about sex myself."

"You are?"

"When I was ten, this fourteen-year-old boy who lived down the block locked me in the basement of his house and made me have sex with him. His younger sister sat there and watched the whole thing."

I didn't know what to say to this. "Wow," I said. I felt a moment of triumph. Finally she had admitted something to me!

And then I remembered the appropriate comment. "That must've been incredibly frightening. I'm sorry you had to go through that."

But the truth was . . . and I know this is going to sound idiotic . . . but the truth was, this tidbit made me even more in awe of her than before. She had experienced the dark side of sex. She'd done too much. That was so much more interesting than not doing enough.

"And the weird thing is," she said, "it really turns me on. Ever since that happened . . . I can have an orgasm if I think back to that. Every single time. It turns me on. Just talking about it now is turning me on."

Needless to say, I was feeling a little tense.

There was an awkward moment, a moment where I didn't know if the conversation was over, or if it would go on to something more.

When suddenly I felt her hand on my thigh. Brushing up my thigh. Making this chill. And my mouth started to water. Not water. Salivate. That word. And then. And then. And then her hand reached under my nightgown (her nightgown, actually—it had tiny pink flowers on it) and her fingers found their way down there, and she put her palm on my . . . my . . . as she would say "cunt" (not that I would say it that way) and then she was inserting her finger inside my vagina (another word I hate) and her finger gently, gently, gently petting me inside—I lay still as a log, paralyzed—but I wanted to see what would happen, but I didn't want to see, and I didn't want to know—and her finger went in deep and then came back out. In deep, then out. I wanted it again . . . I wanted it to stop. Not now . . . not us . . . too much . . . now! This is not. I can't. A woman? When I haven't even had an orgasm . . . with a man . . . and then she leaned over me . . . and started to kiss me. Her lips on my lips! And I turned my head away. I couldn't take it. And I rolled over, rolled away to face the wall, the safety of the hard blank wall. And I heard her sigh—more with annoyance than disappointment, I imagined, at least—and we lay there for a minute in silence. My nightgown pulled down, legs clamped together, eyes squeezed shut.

I tried to tell myself to look at the things other people did all the time that are really shocking and to see that this was nothing, so how could I bother to feel any shame about this at all? But I did feel shame. And I felt shame that I felt shame because it shouldn't have been anything to feel ashamed of.

"Well," she said.

"I'm sorry," I said.

I was sure she knew, anyway, that it was a lack of courage, not interest, on my part. A determination to be "normal." And this was not "normal" for me, not nice little sweet little nice little normal little girl me. Life's ambition: don't do anything that means you aren't normal. Because I already felt so . . . abnormal.

"You know you want it," she finally said.

"But I can't," I finally said.

"Yes you can."

"I hold myself back."

"So stop holding yourself back."

"I can't stop holding myself back. If I give in just a little . . ."

"What?"

"I don't know."

"It's just two bodies."

"I know."

"Two bodies touching."

"I know."

"Two bodies touching and feeling good."

"I know!"

"There's nothing wrong with that. So let yourself feel good."

There is something wrong with that. With feeling good. That's what my mind told me. No matter how much I knew better.

"You can't just tell yourself to feel a certain way and then feel it," I defended myself.

Again, she sighed, exasperated. I felt her giving up on me. I was too slow a student. Hopeless. Feeling safe in the familiarity of my limitations.

"It's so obvious," she said.

"What?"

"And I thought . . ."

Her voice trailed off.

"Thought what?" I pressed.

"I thought you had more of a grip on it . . . enough to be able to write the play . . . but I guess you can see something well enough to turn it into theater without being able to solve it in your own life."

"What exactly are you talking about?"

I knew what she was talking about. I knew she was talking about the fact that I felt so guilty about my sister, that I didn't feel like I deserved to have any pleasure of my own. But I wanted to hear her say it. I felt like it would be soothing to hear her say it. But that's not what she said.

"I'm talking about the fact that you're so afraid of being like your sister that you go to the other extreme."

I had to let that sink in for a moment. I'd never thought of it just like that. "Would you say that again?" It was as if what she said was so true, my brain couldn't grasp it. Like my brain had to grasp itself.

"Well, I didn't know your sister of course. I'm just getting this from the play. But it seems like she was on the promiscuous side, right?"

"Yes."

"And she was a very difficult person to be around, right?"

"Yes."

"She had all these highs and lows. And it was unpredictable."

"Yes."

"And it scares you. You don't want to become like her. Because she was like, out of control. And look what she did. So you go out of your way to be totally *in* control."

I looked up at the ceiling. And I felt my throat tense up. From swallowing the truth. There it was. The story of my life.

"But I mean, God, Jennifer. That doesn't mean you have to completely turn yourself off. You aren't her. You're not going to go bonkers like she did."

"We don't know that."

"Well how are you ever going to find out if you don't test the waters?"

"Maybe it's better not to find out. I mean, there's nothing so wrong with the way I am."

"You're really scared shitless, aren't you."

"My life isn't that bad. I mean, compared to her. I think I'm doing okay."

"Right. Well. Whatever," she said. And she rolled away from me. After a minute she said, "Good night, Jennifer."

"Good night."

And she fell asleep.

And I didn't.

After lying there for ten minutes with my eyes wide open and my body pumped with enough adrenaline to fight off a pack of wild dogs, I got out of her bed, changed into my clothes, went down the stairs past the schmushed dead waterbug, out of her building, onto the street and hailed a cab. I got one immediately, even though it was three o'clock in the morning. And I slid into the backseat and squinched down so the unshaven cabdriver with the beady eyes wouldn't see me because I felt sure that he was toying with the idea of kidnapping me to the Bronx and raping me in an empty parking lot and then dumping my body in a garbage bin outside a Dunkin Donuts.

Fifteen minutes later I was safe, alone, home in my own bed where I promptly fell asleep.

I had just ordered. The waiter had just poured the wine. I had just buttered a piece of bread. I was just about to bring it to my mouth. Just about to take a bite.

But I didn't bring it to my mouth because Peter was leaning forward to tell me something. And I didn't want to be chewing the bread like some cow while he was leaning over telling me something.

"There's something I want to talk with you about," he said. And I put the bread down. I could tell by his face it was important. "I'm glad we could meet in person, because it's better than doing this on the phone."

He looked down at his empty place setting, nervous about what he was going to say. Then he looked back at me, full in the face. His face full of gravity. His blue eyes sort of warm and icy at the same time.

I wondered what it would be. He's gay? Madly in love with me? Sick of the sight of me?

"I don't want you to see this as any kind of attack or criticism."

This sounded bad. I looked down into my bread crust.

"And you know," he went on, "that I believe wholeheartedly in you and your writing . . ."

This sounded really bad. Like maybe that piece of bread would never get to my mouth.

"But I'm thinking that maybe . . . it might be . . . you might want to think about . . . in the second act of the play . . . doing some rewrites."

"You want me . . ."—I felt relieved—"to do some rewrites?" I considered myself to be extremely willing and open when it came to rewrites. Maybe too willing and open, because of a compulsive need to please. And rewriting was usually something I enjoyed. First drafts were hard because they involved exposure and spontaneity and a plunge into the unknown. Rewrites only involved going back over ground that's already been explored. No problem.

"Just in the second act," he said. "And it could just be a matter of a few lines. Important lines, I think. But we aren't talking major changes."

"I've been doing small rewrites all along. That's no big deal, so why are you acting like you're stepping on all my toes?"

"Because. Even though I'm not talking major rewrites in terms of quantity, I do think they're important, and so I know it might seem like I'm contradicting myself because I told you when we began that I thought the play was finished."

"Yes, you did say that . . ."

"But the truth is . . . I was very enamored . . . of the play . . ."

"But now you aren't?"

"I am! But as we've been rehearsing . . ."

"And you've gotten to know me better . . ."

"The play better . . ."

"Me and the play . . ."

"As I've gotten to know you and the play better, I'm realizing something that could help you—"

"I'm not asking for help—"

"Help you to realize the play."

"So now you don't think the play is realized."

"I thought it was. But now I've realized that it's not quite realized."

I couldn't say anything to this.

Stage direction: She does not respond.

"Look," he said. "I know how annoying this must be."

She still does not respond.

"But I'm only trying to help make your play as good as it could possibly be."

"Does this have something to do with Annie's problems with the part?"

"This has to do with my thoughts about your play. That's all. Do you want to hear what I have to say?"

"Do I have a choice?"

"Okay," he said, choosing to forget the bitter tone in my voice. Choosing to ignore the fact that I wanted him to tell me that everything I wrote was brilliant just the way it was and also, by the way, he'd fallen madly and passionately in love with me and knew the secret to unlocking my sexuality and wanted to treat me to a wild night of . . .

"In the third scene," he said, "when Melanie blows up at Julia . . ."—and here he paused for dramatic effect—"does she say everything that she needs to say?"

I thought for a moment. Actually, I took a moment to make it appear like I was thinking for a moment. "Yes. She does."

"Are you sure?"

"Yes. She says a lot. She blows up. She says horrible things!"

"Are they really so horrible?"

"Yes!"

"So horrible that the audience believes that they're bad enough to drive Julia to kill herself?"

"They don't have to be that horrible. They only have to be

horrible enough for Melanie to believe that she's driven Julia to kill herself."

"I disagree," he said.

He of all people, I thought, of all guilty souls, should know what I was talking about.

"Fine," I said. "So disagree."

"I'm not saying that you can't leave it like it is . . ."

"Thank you."

"But I'm thinking you could get a lot more out of it . . . if you made it so blatantly hostile that we truly believe Melanie could've pushed Julia over the edge."

"I think the audience *does* believe that. I think her words *are* that hostile."

"They may seem hostile to you. But you happen to be a very sensitive person. To most people . . ."

"How can you say this? You had no problem with this before rehearsals. You're just buckling under Annie's complaining because she's not smart enough to understand the part!"

"First of all, Annie is a very intelligent person and second of all, I wouldn't do that."

"Okay, not that she isn't smart enough, just that she's never experienced something like this in her own life so she can't relate—"

"That's not what's going on here."

"Kelly said something to you, didn't she."

"No."

"Something about the layers, the layers needing to be peeled away. I bet you all had a nice powwow, didn't you, last week when I had to miss rehearsal. I bet you all had fun sitting there picking apart my play!"

(I knew I was sounding a tad hysterical but I couldn't help myself.)

"Kelly hasn't said one word to me about your play. Did she say something to you?"

I was silent for a moment, thinking about how they were ganging up on me because they were insecure because they were afraid they wouldn't be able to get it together in time so I had to be the fall guy.

"Yes," I admitted, "Kelly was complaining to me about something. But the complaints of two actresses who can't even get their lines memorized when we're about to open doesn't count."

"Surely you can see that if three different people are saying more or less the same thing then maybe you should listen."

I couldn't speak. I was too upset. It seemed like this particular criticism really, really, bothered me. Like it was hitting on something that I did not want to hear. That I . . . well, no, not me—that Melanie had to be meaner, fiercer, let loose with all her feelings no matter what the consequences. She had to let her anger out. Like Julia. Like Diana. Diana, who I tried so hard to be unlike. Just as Kelly had said the night before. I had to keep control. Because she was so out of control. And that was how I survived. That's what kept me safe from her fate. And safe from her, and her mood swings. By being sensitive enough for the both of us. Able to see both points of view.

I would never say those cruel things. And Melanie wouldn't say them. She might think them, but she would never say them, and certainly not to Julia, who had to be protected from such feelings; couldn't they see that?

And then, as if he was reading my thoughts, Peter said, "In a play . . . people say things. They say things that usually don't get said. Sometimes I think that's the whole point of a play. For people to come and hear the words that are too painful to be spoken."

He took a sip of his beer, then stared down into it. I took a sip of water. Looked at my buttered piece of bread, bound for the garbage can back in the restaurant kitchen.

He put his hand on my hand.

"I know this is hard to take in, Jennifer. Sleep on it. Mull it over. See if something comes to you. I know it's hard. It means you have to feel through an experience that you'd rather not feel through. But that's what writing is all about, isn't it?"

I couldn't speak. He was being so gentle with me, and I felt like striking him in the face.

And sitting on his lap. And resting my head against his chest. And crying in his arms.

"Yes," I said. "I suppose so."

But inside I was thinking, no. That's not what writing is about. Writing is about pouring your heart out and exposing yourself to other people and then having people repay you with criticisms because you managed to express something that made them uncomfortable.

But I didn't say that because somewhere inside of me I knew that it was very possible that I was utterly overreacting. And horribly defensive. And just plain wrong.

The waiter brought our food. I looked at my chicken with no appetite as I thanked Peter for his feedback. "I'll think about it," I said. And then I forced myself to eat.

Chapter

8

All I could think about after dinner as I walked up Eighth Avenue was how much I hated them all. Hated them! Their snug little circle of criticism! Annie with her superior-to-Melanie attitude. Kelly with her oozing sexuality. Peter with his self-righteous know-it-all arrogance. Well I wouldn't listen to them. A writer has to be strong! You can't let people gang up on you with their opinions and tell you what to write. This was my story and I was telling it my way—the way I knew to tell it. Just because they didn't know the first thing about telling their own stories (all of them swimming around in their own little fish bowls) they wanted to tell me how to tell mine.

Except . . . this anger. This hate. A hate so strong I wanted to kill all of them. I could use this hate, I sensed. In her speech. And make it stronger.

No. I would not listen to them. They were polluting me! Melanie wouldn't talk like that. She might wish something horrible about another person but she could never be so mean to their faces. She was too sure that it would destroy her, destroy the other person—she would hold it in!

But wasn't that the point? That her words could destroy, that her feelings could destroy? And how could the audience know what she was thinking and feeling if she held it all in?

That's what Annie had said.

But she didn't hold it in. She did say some pretty bad things to Julia.

But were they not bad enough? I had to be true to Melanie. If I wasn't, then what was the point?

I wished I had the scene in front of me. I would look at the lines, see exactly what she said. Maybe all it needed was one line more, maybe two, just like he'd said. Sometimes you got a big criticism like this, but that was all it took.

No! I wouldn't let them win. Just because they didn't understand, I would not cater to their ignorance.

But if they didn't understand, how would the audience? What good was a play if I was the only one who understood it?

But was I? Maybe it didn't speak to them, but it would speak to others like me. God knows there were a lot of plays out there that didn't appeal to me because I couldn't identify. And here I was, writing a play for people like me . . . scared, hesitant, inhibited, bottled up people like me. And all these pushy theater people were trying to get me to change her and make her like them. Well I wouldn't. I wouldn't let them push me around. I would be strong!

Or was I being weak?

Why didn't I know?!

With my brain buzzing, I covered twenty blocks in no time, hardly noticing where I was. I reached my apartment and vaguely thought of looking in my script. But instead, I fell into bed, telling myself I had every right to. After all, I was still exhausted from the night before with Kelly. As I snuggled under my covers, I told myself I didn't want to look over my play, I didn't want to think about, I wished it didn't exist. Just wanted to fall into a deep sleep far away from thoughts and feelings because other people ... other people ... they always let you down.

I woke up the next morning with regret. I didn't want to leave the sleep world behind. Didn't want to think about my play. But I knew that I would have to force myself to sit down with it. Look at the lines and see if anything that Peter said would make sense to me now that I was a little more calm. Was this rising to the occasion? Or buckling under pressure. I didn't know.

First, breakfast. I walked to the Westway, the diner where Peter and I first met, with a copy of the play just in case I could stand to look at it. I also brought a copy of the *Times* just to let myself know that I didn't have to look at my play if I didn't want to. I ordered a blueberry muffin and coffee. It was one of their big beautiful, blueberry muffins that I always ogled in the showcase and never let myself order because they were too fattening. But today I got one. It was a bribe, pure and simple. Eat the muffin—look at the play. That would be the deal. Unless I didn't want to.

It was Monday morning and people around me were hustling to get to work. I had the day off, and this was the day of Kelly's audition, so there was no rehearsal. That meant I had the luxury of time. Hours of uninterrupted time with no obligations to the outside world where I could look at my play that I didn't want to look at and figure out if Melanie had said all she needed to say.

But I couldn't get myself to open it up.

I read the headlines on my newspaper. All the Dot Coms were failing and there was an earthquake in South America and another suburban teenager had killed some popular kids, but none of it mattered. It had nothing to do with me.

I should get out my play. My play that had to do with me. But maybe that was the problem. Maybe the play had only to do with me. Maybe no one else in the world could care less about this character. Because I was a freak. I was the only person alive in the world who was like me.

I should write a play about a nymphomaniac cheerleader who gets trapped in an earthquake in South America. Then they would care.

I drank my coffee, which tasted a little too much like dishwater, and ate the muffin, which was too dry. It was made with canned blueberries and corn syrup, and was totally disappointing. I should've gotten a bagel with butter as usual. Now I was stuck with wasted calories. Wasted calories and a wasted life.

But finally, thank god, the lousy coffee started to kick in. A mental zing. A curiosity to see the words. The words were my friends. Life was comforting and familiar around the words. I forced myself to put the play in front of my face and open it up. No obligation to read it. Just find the page the scene was on. And place it in front of my eyes. No obligation to do anything whatsoever.

There it was. The conversation between Melanie and Julia at the end of the third scene. The last time they saw each other before Julia killed herself. The blowout that Diana and I never had.

I didn't want to read it. Didn't want to think about it. Anything would be preferable to having to think about what those two characters needed to say in that scene.

I looked up towards the door of the coffee shop. I looked at the pay phone by the door. No one came in. No one came out. I stared at a fly that landed on my table. Watched it rub its two little stick legs together, like it was an evil scientist planning to take over the world. I took another bite of lousy muffin and another sip of lousy coffee and looked back down at the page. The typewritten lines stared back at me. I was prepared to hate every single one of them.

The waiter came by. More lousy coffee? Yes. He poured. I

added cream. Took another sip. Forced my eyes to the page. What does she say? What does Melanie say? She's finally talking about the wedding. Her anger about the wedding. I made myself read.

Melanie: *"I was trying to get you to reassure me. To give me your encouragement to go ahead with the wedding. But you wouldn't do that, would you."*

Julia: *"If you had that many doubts about the man you were going to marry—"*

Melanie: *"Not him. You! You seemed so upset, and I wanted to protect you, and I guess I even played him down a little because I didn't want you to be jealous. And you took advantage of that and twisted me all up inside and I just couldn't be happy knowing that if I got married it would make you unhappy!"*

I took a sip of coffee and kept reading.

Julia: *"So you sacrificed yourself and then you blamed me for your entire life. Because it's so much easier than taking responsibility for yourself."*

Melanie: *"You think it's easy? Going through life like some kind of deformed hunchback, always trying to stay lower, stay lower, so I never overtake you—so I always let you win?"*

Julia: *"Let me win?! You don't even compete. Because you know you'd always lose. And it's so much easier to wallow around in self-pity than to pull your own weight, isn't it."*

Melanie: *"You want me to pull my own weight? Fine, I'll pull it. You can't stay here!"*

Julia: *"I've lost my lease. I'll end up on the street. But you don't give a fuck, do you, all you care about is yourself!"*

Melanie: *"How can you say that? Who lent you money when you quit your job and couldn't go a day without getting high? Who stayed up with you night after night because you went off your medications and thought the spiders on your shower curtain were going to eat you alive?!"*

Julia: *"Fine. Enjoy having your apartment all to yourself, Melanie. And don't worry, I'll never ask you for anything, ever again."*
Melanie: *"That sounds good to me!"*
Julia: *"Have a nice life, Melanie. I dare you to have a nice life!"*
And she exits, slamming the door behind her.

I read the passage once more. Melanie did finally stand up to Julia. But it was true, she was still holding back. Still protecting Julia from her feelings instead of letting them all out.

I felt something uncomfortable in my gut. How can she tell the sister . . . tell the sister . . . when her sister is so vulnerable, so miserable, so miserable she's about to . . . not that she knows she's about to . . . but how can she tell her how she really feels? It would be too horrible. Too horrible to know that you've said those things and then she went and . . .

But isn't that the point? To make the drama as horrible as possible?

I froze for a moment. Thought back to my own sister. The reality of my own sister, who was not these words on the page here. She actually existed. She actually ended her own life. And it wasn't my fault, of course, but it was, it was, I couldn't help but feel like it was my fault because I . . . I what?! Because I what?! What did I think I did?!

The tears welled up and started to spill out. But I had to stop them, stifle the sobs, because other people must not see you cry (Why don't people sob in public all the time—how do people manage to be on such an even keel?). So I quickly wiped my eyes, but the tears kept coming, I couldn't hold them in, and my chest heaved with sobs and I wanted to scream out to the entire restaurant how I HATED her! Hated her for making me feel this way! For making me miserable my entire life, always feeling her misery as if I was the reason for it. As if feeling her misery would make life easier for her, but it never did it, she just continued with her self-destructive ways and made me hate her and—

"Hate you," I wrote. *"Hate you for making me feel this way. Miserable my whole life, as if I was the cause. But it's not my fault. It has never been my fault. Because you have never been happy no matter what I do. There was always something making you angry, some injustice, some reason to yell and scream and throw a fit and make everyone around you feel unhappy like we were all doing something wrong. But it wasn't us, it had nothing to do with anything any of us ever did—it was you! Selfish, egotistical, mentally unbalanced chemically screwed-up YOU! So don't come asking me for favors, Julia. I'm sick of you and your problems. I've spent my life tiptoeing my own needs around you and it never seems to do any good because you always end up in trouble anyway, so just stop asking for help and leave me alone!"*

I put down my pen. My hand was sore from gripping it. I read through the rest of the scene.

Julia: *"Fine. Enjoy having your apartment all to yourself, Melanie. And don't worry, I'll never ask you for anything, ever again."*

Melanie: *"That sounds good to me!"*

Julia: *"Have a nice life, Melanie. I dare you to have a nice life!"*

And she slams the door and exits.

And we never see each other again.

I took a deep breath and let it out. The speech was overwritten and would need some editing. But it would lead so much better into the final scene, where Julia comes back as a ghost haunting her. Finally. Melanie had said everything she needed to say.

I showed up early at the theater for Tuesday rehearsal with the new lines. I didn't want to admit to "defeat" for having taken their advice—even if it did make the play better. But I felt embarrassed that I had been so resistant. And I looked forward to seeing Peter be pleased.

"I guess you win," I said, handing him the new page and looking properly sheepish.

"If you made it better, then you're the one who wins," he said back.

I wished I didn't feel like "the good little girl playwright" doing as she was told. But they were my words, I had to remind myself, and they had come out of me. And at least they weren't "good little girl" words.

"Thanks," I said.

"I didn't do anything."

"You pushed me."

"That was easy. I couldn't stop myself."

"Sorry I was so grouchy about it the other night," I said. "I guess it sort of ruined the evening."

"There will be other evenings."

He gave me a little smile, and I felt a wave of happiness, and it was at that moment that Kelly made her entrance. She looked tired.

"Hello, you two." She looked back and forth between us trying to size up the moment. "Have a good weekend?"

"Not bad," Peter said. "And you?"

"It had its ups and downs."

I wasn't sure if she was embarrassed over the other night. In her bed. I didn't think it was likely. To her it was probably nothing. But to me, it still felt awkward.

"How'd your audition go?" I asked.

"My agent called this morning. They didn't want me."

"I'm sorry," I said, feeling immense relief.

"It's rough," Peter said.

"Rejection sucks," she said, looking straight at me. I couldn't help but wonder if she was making some kind of reference to our own little tryout, though I couldn't really believe she could feel rejected by me. Especially since she knew it was my inhibitions that held me back. Especially since it was Peter she really wanted.

"Well, they don't know what they're missing," I said.

"I guess it wasn't meant to be," she said.

"If it's any consolation," Peter said, "we're happy not to lose you."

"Yeah," I agreed. "We're grateful for that."

"And I would've felt horrible dropping out of the play. So at least we were all saved from that crisis."

She smiled at me. But it wasn't a very sincere smile, and I refrained from saying, *Are you kidding? You would've been out of here faster than I can say, "But we don't have an understudy!"*

Just then Annie arrived, and I handed her the new page. She started reading it over immediately.

When she was done, she looked up at me and said, "Cool."

Finally, things were becoming real. That is, the illusion was becoming real. A guy named Felix was on a ladder hanging the lights. A sound person was hired to record the few sound cues we needed and some music for intermission. The construction of the set was almost finished, and the flats were being painted to look like the shoddy walls of a run-down studio walk-up. We were having a small problem with the fake window that kept spontaneously sliding shut (when my sister's ghost was coming in and out?). And Lucas, the prop master, was starting to bring things in to make the apartment look real and lived in. He actually lugged, with Peter's help, an incredibly heavy iron radiator from the flea market a few blocks away. And when they set it up against the wall, it made the whole apartment seem authentic.

We still had to find the right bedspread for the bed, and Lucas asked me what kind of pictures Melanie would have on her wall. I considered telling him I could bring something from home—I had a Matisse print of a young girl that seemed perfect. But then I realized it would be creepy to see my own things on the set, so I told him to check out the posters at the gift shop at the Museum of Modern Art.

Annie and Kelly could now muddle their way through the play without scripts in hand. And Carol sat in the front row giving them the occasional missed cue. I sat in my usual spot in the back row staying out of the way as much as possible. It was like I was a child who needed to be extra good while they did the hard work of keeping the marriage together until opening night.

Later that week, Peter took me out for a drink after rehearsal. I wanted him to be happy with how things were going, but he looked tired and worried.

"It's going well," I said, wanting to reassure him.

"Do you think so?"

"Yes, don't you?"

"Something's not right. I feel a definite tension in the air."

"But that's good. That's to be expected."

"I know what you're saying. But I'm sensing something . . ."

"Annie is finally coming around with her part, don't you think?"

"Yes. It's Julia—Kelly—that I'm worried about. I'm getting some kind of bad vibe from her, but I can't put my finger on it."

I kept my mouth shut. No use mentioning that (speaking of fingers) she had, like, stuck hers up my vagina or anything.

"I gave her a few directions today that she ignored," Peter went on. "It's not like her. Now she seems intent on doing her own thing."

"I do like what she's doing in general."

"But haven't you noticed she has this air of defiance now? I tell her to move upstage and she moves downstage. I tell her to pause before a certain line and she repeatedly skips the pause."

"I guess I did notice," I said. Now I wondered if something had transpired between the two of them. Something he wasn't telling me. Maybe he'd rejected her and she was going to take it out on all of us.

"They're small things," Peter said, "but they add up."

"Has she said anything to you? Approached you about any . . . you know, concerns?"

"No."

I noticed he didn't mention that she'd asked him out the previous weekend. But then I didn't mention I'd been with her, either. "Maybe it's just that she has so much to think about now that they're getting off book and adding the blocking too."

"Nah. Kelly is a pro. She has no trouble coordinating her lines with the blocking. I think she's doing it on purpose."

"You mean like she's challenging your authority?"

"Maybe. This is one of the risks you take working with someone you don't know. It could be her way of dealing with the pressure."

"Or not dealing with it," I said. "And we're at her mercy. You can give her all sorts of direction, but in the end she's the one who's going to be up there and she'll do what she wants. We can't even fire her in our situation . . ."

"Ultimately, it's the actors who make the play or ruin it."

"We're totally in their hands." I dumped ketchup on my plate. "And in the end, when the play is being performed, the audience perceives the play as if the actors made the whole thing up. Not the writer, and certainly not the director, who always stays invisible."

"Most people don't even know how to tell what the hell a director does!"

"Awww," I said, "you're so unappreciated."

I gave him a pretend pout of sympathy and felt the urge to lean over and kiss his beleaguered cheek. But thank god I didn't, because at that moment Kelly and Annie walked into the bar. They saw us sitting there cozily, nodded hello, smiled, and waved. We nodded, smiled and waved back. And they went to their own table.

"Well," Peter said, "it's good to see they finally bonded."

"I didn't know they had." I couldn't help but feel a little left out. I wondered if Kelly would make some kind of move on Annie now. Well, that was fine. Better Annie than Peter.

"They've probably got a lot to complain about," Peter said. "Especially me."

"You're being paranoid."

"It's not paranoia when they really do hate you."

"They don't hate you! On the contrary . . . Kelly would just love to hop into bed with you. She told me so."

That slipped out.

Why did I say that?

I really wished I had not said that.

"Well . . . that's interesting. But I make it a policy never to get involved with actresses."

I was dying to ask if he had a policy of never getting involved with playwrights.

"But that's classic for the actress and the director to have an affair," I said.

"Classically idiotic. Then she expects you to cast her in every single thing you're directing. No thank you."

"I think they understand when a part isn't right for them." (Meaning I, as a playwright, would not expect him to direct every single play that I write.)

"But almost every part in a play has an ingenue," he went on, "and if she's an ingenue, then there's a potential part in almost every play ever written!"

"I guess."

"Anyway," he concluded, "actresses are too flighty."

"But they can also be entertaining."

What was I trying to do? Get him into bed with her?

"What are you trying to do? Get me to go to bed with her?"

"No, of course not."

"Good."

We looked over at their table. They looked over at us and smiled. We smiled back.

"Let's go," Peter said. "Are you ready?"

"Sure."

We stopped at their table on the way out.

"Nice rehearsal today," Peter said.

"Thank you, Mr. Director," Annie said.

Kelly just smiled. So did I.

"Kelly and I are going to run lines together tonight," Annie said.

"Great," Peter said. "We'll see you tomorrow."

As Peter and I walked out of Rosie O'Grady's, I could feel Kelly's eyes on my back. Now that she'd seen me all cozy with him, I feared she wouldn't feel very much like learning her lines. I decided it would be a good idea to call her. Let her know there was nothing going on between him and me. Maybe it seemed like there was, I'd reassure her, but really, we were just friends. That's all.

Chapter
9

But I didn't quite get around to having that conversation with her. And a few nights later, Peter and I were sunk into my sofa watching *Saturday Night Live* but not really watching.

"What are you thinking?" he asked.

"I'm thinking about how I have all these ancestors going back hundreds and hundreds of years and I don't even know their names. I know nothing about them. And they don't know anything about me."

"That would be hard for them to know something about you."

"But we share the same genes!"

"So?"

His arm was over my shoulder. Our thighs were touching. But I couldn't quite relax into him. I couldn't quite do it.

"Of course everyone has video cameras now," I said, "and so our ancestors will know what we look like and sound like and move like."

"You mean your descendants."

"Right."

"If they can stand to watch. There's nothing so boring as watching video home movies."

"Yeah, but it's there. If they want to see. It's funny to think that we're the first generation that gets that immortality. My great, great grandchildren will know that I slouch."

"And that you're beautiful."

"Thanks." I blushed. I'm a sucker for comments like that.

"I can't imagine myself as a mother," I said. Deflecting. Always deflecting his flirtation even though I was ready to be the mother of his children then and there so why bother pretending otherwise?

"Why not?"

"Because you have to scold them. And I can't even yell when I'm angry. I'm much more likely to cry. So how am I going to discipline them?"

"I'm sure you can be angry if you need to be."

"I don't think so."

"Go ahead and try."

"You mean be angry? Right now?"

"Yeah. Act it. Once you've faked something then it's a lot easier to actually be it when the time comes."

"I don't believe that."

"Let's say one of your kids just threw the only copy of your new play down a garbage chute."

"But it doesn't matter because it would be on my computer so I can just print out another copy."

"You wrote it out by hand. It was a labor of love."

"No one does that anymore!"

"And that's why you're so angry—because you put so much time and energy into creating that thing and your bratty little kid just threw it down the garbage chute."

"Okay." I narrowed my eyes and looked downwards towards my imaginary child. "You threw my new play down the garbage chute?" I drew my eyebrows towards my nose and tensed my mouth with meanness. "Well. You know what I'm gonna do about that?!" I tried to think of something. What would I do? "I'll write another play. That one wasn't very good anyway. So don't worry about it, okay?"

Peter groaned.

"See? I can't do it."

"Come on! It was a great play. It would've won you the Pulitzer Prize! And she threw it away because she didn't want to share you with anyone. Go ahead."

"Okay." I breathed out. I wasn't into this. "I am very angry with you. Now say you're sorry or I'll eat up all your cookies while you're sleeping!"

He looked at me skeptically. "Maybe when you actually have children you'll learn to be scary out of necessity."

"I bet you'll be good at yelling at your children after dealing with actors all the time."

"I suppose that's true."

"Not that you yell at them."

"Oh yes I do."

"I haven't heard you."

"Just wait till the last week of rehearsals."

"Uh oh."

And we looked back at the TV. *Saturday Night Live* was ending. It was getting late. He was still there. With me. On my couch. My eyes stayed glued to the screen. Beer commercials. Jeeps. Call 1-800-M-A-T-T-R-E-S. Keep the focus on anything but us. And what might happen next.

Next.

His arm around me. I couldn't focus. I felt drunk even though I wasn't—like my head was full of heavy syrup that was sedating me so that I fell into every crevice of his body and the inside of my vagina (there must be a better word) was tingling with anticipation though I had no idea if he was going to make a move on me or not and even if he was I couldn't be sure I would go through with having sex with him. I hadn't had sex since Marc, and he seemed like from another lifetime. Plus how could I do this to Kelly? She'd be angry, and I wasn't sure if I could take that, and the last thing we needed was an angry actress—

"Do you mind if I turn the TV off?" Peter asked.

"No," I said.

"You look tense." He sat down next to me again.

"I do?" I swallowed.

"Would you like a massage?"

"Okay."

So I lay face down on the sofa and he sat on my bottom. (I almost said "butt," but that word is so unromantic, and "ass" is even worse.)

I'd like to say that I ripped my shirt off and my bra too and felt proud of my hot sexy little body. But that would not quite sound authentic at this point. The truth is, I didn't want to let him see me without my clothes on. And so I felt relieved when he went ahead and slipped his hands up under my shirt and then proceeded to give me this wonderful massage. I would call it "exquisite" if I used that word, but I don't. He touched me just where I wanted to be touched, with just the right amount of pressure, very symmetrical, very reassuring. Just thinking about it almost puts me in a trance. This was easy. I could stay totally passive. Didn't have to show myself one bit, just receive in silence.

But the idea of sex loomed. Okay, this was nothing new. But with Marc, I'd felt patient with myself, chalked it up to youth and inexperience. Now, as I felt the same old inhibitions closing in on me, I felt like I was beyond ridiculous. A freak. I had to get over this. And I really wanted to, with Peter, I wanted to stop laying all these trips on myself. Stop trying to keep control. Like Kelly had said. But I could not imagine transforming our relationship into something so . . . making it . . . what was that word . . . ?

Carnal.

That's the word. I couldn't make it carnal with him.

With myself.

Come to think of it, I don't know exactly what that word means. Carnal. But it does seem to mean what I felt I wasn't. I'm going to look it up.

Carnal. French. That figures. Fourteenth century. Marked by sexuality. FLESHLY. ANIMAL. SENSUAL. Yes. But here, even more to the point. *Relating to or given to crude bodily pleasures and appetites . . . often connotes derogatorily an action or manifestation of man's lower nature.* That's it. I had lost that carnal lower nature thing somewhere along the way. Snuffed it out of myself. Because my sister had more than enough for both of us.

Except lots of people had it. And they were happy and well-adjusted. I knew that. In an abstract way. But I couldn't know it enough to really believe it. If I could just get my body to know it (and forget about my stupid head) then maybe I could get around this whole stupid problem. Because my lower nature had to be in me somewhere still, and I wanted it. I wanted my lower nature back!

After awhile he stopped the massage and lay down sort of half on top of me and half on the couch. My eyes were closed, but I could feel his breathing on my nose.

I reassured myself that he didn't want sex anyway, not with me; why would he want that with me? He just wanted to give me a nice massage, that was all. And now he was done and he would go home. The one he wanted to have sex with, that would be Kelly. Not someone with a zillion hang-ups like me, which he must realize. And if he didn't realize, he certainly would soon enough . . .

And then he slid down, wedging himself between me and the back of the couch. And I started to turn towards him. I couldn't help myself. And his lips were on my lips. And he kissed me. Softly. Warmly. And our bodies were pressed right up against each other. And I wanted to melt into him. (It's hard to avoid clichés at moments like this.) I could feel his erection pressing up against me (!) and my leg went over his leg, and I wanted him inside me (as they say) and his lips were like (can I think of one more lousy cliché here?) velvet, flower petals, some kind of mushy fruit, I don't know—they were like lips!

I hate sex scenes. I mean why should anyone try to conjure up a sex scene? Everyone who's had sex knows what it feels like, and anyone who hasn't (is there anyone left?) can certainly imagine what it's like (it's always better the way you imagine it anyway, isn't it?). So in any case. The point is. We kissed.

And there, as if on cue, was my sister hovering over me. "You think you're going to enjoy yourself? You think *I'm* enjoying myself? How dare you try to enjoy yourself . . . !"

Which made it hard to relax.

But I did my best. Tried to get her out of my mind. Blank my mind, just think about Peter, focus on the here and now, the him and me, physical sensations, nothing to feel guilty about, just two bodies feeling good, making each other feel good, nothing wrong with that. And I really thought that we were going to go "all the way" (and that I was going to let myself) but then he stopped. And he sat up. And he said "excuse me." And he went to the bathroom.

So I sat up too. And I tried to collect myself. As if my body had spilled all over the couch and I had to stuff myself back into my clothes to make a solid mass again.

A few minutes later—which I spent staring at the television set trying not to think about the fact that when men pee they need to hold their penises—he came out of the bathroom. And he sat down next to me and put his arm around me and leaned towards me like he was going to kiss me again, and my anxiety overtook me and I said, of all things (and I know what an idiot this makes me) "Maybe you should get going."

"Really?" he asked.

"Yes."

"Is that what you want?"

"Well . . . I just think that maybe . . . we shouldn't . . . at this point . . . right now."

I was aware that I was disappointing myself, him, the world.

"Why shouldn't we?" he asked. "At this point. Right now."

And I said, stupidly, "It seems like a director shouldn't get involved with a playwright."

It was a moment before he answered.

"Oh."

"You know," I continued. Lamely. I mean, did I think I was being funny or something? "Because then they'll just want you to direct all their plays."

"Are you being sarcastic?" he asked.

"What?"

"Because we are involved."

"We are?"

"Aren't we?"

"Well . . ." I said, stupidly (if I may judge myself impartially), "I don't know."

I don't know, I said? When I should've been utterly delighted?

"Okay. Well, then. I don't know either."

Pause. Silence. Interminable length of time during which I should've said something that would've fixed the situation but failed to.

It was Peter who broke the silence. "Maybe I'd better go."

"You don't have to go."

"I probably should."

Just because I'm too freaked out to have sex doesn't mean you have to go, I was thinking.

"What are you thinking?" he asked.

You could just sleep here. And not have sex. Or whatever. Because . . . you know . . . I'm in love with you. I know it doesn't seem like it by the way I'm behaving, but I am . . .

But I couldn't come out with the words. Like he would think I was weird to want him to stay and not have sex. Everyone wants to have sex, right? Morning, noon, nighttime and every time in-between. So what was wrong with me? Why did I have to be me? Why couldn't I have been anyone other than me?!

"Nothing," I said.

"Okay. Well. I'm exhausted," he said. "And tomorrow is a big day."

"Yes."

"And I need to get some rest."

You could get some rest here, I wanted to say . . . but my mouth didn't move. And he got his things together, and I walked him to the door thinking, *He should try harder. He should try harder to stay.*

"These last few days of rehearsal are going to be rough," he said.

But of course, he couldn't try harder because we were two guilty souls. Two guilty souls who didn't deserve . . .

"I hope Annie and Kelly are working on their lines," I said, returning to the safe subject of my play, the production, anything but us, "because if they don't have them soon . . ."

"Don't worry, it always looks bleak just before you're about to open."

"Like nothing's going to come together."

"And then it does."

"Hopefully."

We stood at the door. *Tell him you love him*, a little voice urged me.

"I have to make a lot of phone calls in the morning," he was saying. "A bunch of producers I should call. It's important we get them in to see the play. We don't want to do all this work and have nothing to show for it, right?"

"Sometimes I think that's the hardest part. Getting people in to see it." *Tell him*, the little voice said, *you didn't mean to stop him, it was just your irrational fears.*

"Especially the people who can do something for you."

"Making those calls. I know that's a pain."

"Yeah, it's a pain."

It's especially a pain, the little voice said, *since you didn't have sex with him.*

"Thank you for doing that," I said.

"I want to see this thing get moved as much as you do."

"Yes. It would be great."

I made myself meet his eyes. Maybe he would see, in my eyes, how much I wanted him. "So I'll see you tomorrow."

"See you tomorrow," he said. And he left. And I shut the door. And my little voice stopped saying anything. I guess it was pissed off, so it was giving me the silent treatment.

Chapter

10

It was three days before we were set to open. The theater was hot. There was air-conditioning, but it was noisy and mostly ineffective. Cast and crew were tense. They were trying to coordinate the lighting cues with the blocking. But everyone was making mistakes, and nothing was working. Kelly's performance, in particular, was flat.

It was hard to say if it was because of the tedium of having spoken the words of the play so many times over and over, day after day, with no audience there to respond. And once there were people in the seats, she would raise the level of her performance up a few notches. Or maybe it was some kind of residual weirdness between me and her. Or frustration over Peter. Or maybe she was simply self-destructing because that's what she did. Or all of the above.

I watched Peter trying to get a performance out of her without antagonizing her in the process, but he was losing his patience.

"Could you take this scene again?" he asked. "And this time, Kelly, could you put some energy into it? I know it's hot today and you're all feeling tired . . ."

"I feel fine," she said, quite casually.

"You were slow with your cues," he said, "and your volume was too low."

I could hear the tension in his voice. He usually took care to talk calmly to the actors, but now, just as he had predicted, his equilibrium was starting to crack.

Kelly pretended not to notice. "Fine," she said pleasantly.

They took the scene again. But this time she went to the opposite extreme, rushing her lines and almost shouting them out.

"Kelly," Peter interrupted. "Are you not feeling well today?"

"I thought I was following your instructions," she responded, feigning innocence.

Annie was looking distressed. Nothing she could do. I considered leaving. Done well, the scenes could be emotionally wrenching. Done badly, they were intolerable. But if this was going to turn into a good fight, I didn't want to miss it.

"Take it from the top of the third scene," Peter said.

The actresses reluctantly took their places and began again.

I decided not to listen, and shut them out as much as possible. I didn't want to think about Melanie and Julia. I wanted to think about Peter. He'd basically ignored me all day. In his case, I had no doubt it was because of residual weirdness from the other night. But of course, he was also preoccupied with the play and once we opened, I hoped, we would continue where we left off. And I would do better the next time, I told myself, I would have to make myself do better.

It occurred to me that in the past couple weeks I'd managed to reject the overtures of the two people I was enamored with.

Finally, they were onto the fourth and last scene of the play. This scene would stand alone after intermission. Julia has killed herself and comes back to haunt Melanie. It was the same scene that had seemed so heartbreaking in the very first read-through, when they had acted it so well I was brought to tears. But today, Kelly wouldn't have made the first round on Star Search.

For one thing, she still didn't have her lines. So they had to keep stop/starting, stop/starting, stop/starting. And when she could deliver a line, the rhythm was off. Peter reminded them that the pace, especially in this scene, had to be very fast, with the lines volleyed back and forth with intensity. Because in a sense, the "ghost" was the inside of Melanie's head, and she was talking to herself.

Melanie: *"I called the next day."*

Julia: *"Not this again."*

Melanie: *"And I left a message."*

Julia: *"We know, we know."*

Melanie: *"And I told you I changed my mind and you could move in."*

Julia: *"But you were too late."*

"Faster!" Peter interrupted. "I don't want to hear any airspace between the lines! Melanie, overlap, 'And I told you I changed my mind' over her second 'we know.' Again!"

Melanie: *"I called the next day."*

Julia: *"Not this again."*

Melanie: *"And I left a message."*

Julia: *"We know, we know."*

Melanie: *"And I told you I changed my mind and you could move in."*

Julia: *"But you were too late."*

Melanie: *"Two days passed. You didn't call. I got a bad feeling."*

Kelly asked for her line. Carol fed it. "'You can go over and over—'"

Julia: *"You can go over and over it in your mind—"*

Melanie: *"A very bad feeling."*

Julia: *"But it won't turn out any differently. The ending will always be the same."*

They stumbled through another page and started to reach the climax of the scene. I leaned forward, listening for the build.

Melanie: *"So I walked over to your place."*
Julia: *"You really should've taken a cab."*
Melanie: *"I went down the streets very slowly."*
Julia: *"I could've been writhing on the floor in pain."*
Melanie: *"And looked at everything very carefully."*
"Drive it!" Peter urged.
Julia: *"Breathing my last breaths."*
Melanie: *"I had the feeling I would never look at anything the same again."*
Julia: *"And what did you see Melanie, tell me what you saw."*
Melanie: *"The apartment was its usual mess."*
Kelly broke the spell. "I'm sorry, line?" she asked.

This section should've come easy. Kelly, the self-proclaimed "quick study" had to be doing it on purpose.

Carol fed her the line. "'If I'd known you were—'"
Julia: *"If I'd known you were coming I would've cleaned up."*
Melanie: *"You knew I had the key—"*
Carol: "'You knew I would come, you knew I had the key.'"
"Sorry," Annie said. "Fuck."
"Just take it back a line, Kelly. 'If I'd known you were coming—'"
Julia: *"If I'd known you were coming I would've cleaned up."*
Melanie: *"You knew I would come, you knew I had the key. I walked in the door. The apartment was silent. There was an open yogurt on the table next to the rocking chair. Mold growing in the yogurt. A library book propped open on the coffee table.* The Andy Warhol Diaries. *You were halfway through."*
Julia: *"Boring."*
Melanie: *"I called out your name. No answer. Went slowly into the bedroom. The kitty ran past. Your bed was unmade. Not surprising. There's still the hope that you were angry with me, and you've*

*just gone on a walk, and you'll be coming up the stairs to your apart-
ment any second, and I'll say, 'God! Julia! Where have you been? I
was starting to think . . . !' "*

Julia: *"And I would say, Melanie. I'm so happy to see you."*

I leaned forward in my seat, tensing for what I knew was
coming next. But Kelly broke the rhythm.

"Line?"

I knew she knew that line. She'd quoted it to me the night
she made me dinner at her apartment.

Carol read it off the script. " 'If I'd known you were coming,
I would've made you some dinner. Your favorite pasta, with
sweet Italian sausage!' "

Julia: *"If I'd known you were coming, I would've made you some
dinner. Your favorite pasta, with sweet Italian sausage!"*

Melanie: *"You enjoy torturing me, don't you—"*

Annie was midway through her line when suddenly Kelly
stopped and looked at Peter.

"I'm sorry," Kelly said, "but I'm having a problem with
this."

"You bet you're having a problem—you're still fumbling
your lines!"

Kelly threw her script on the floor. "That's because the
lines don't make any sense!"

I shifted in my seat. What was she doing?

Peter tried to keep his voice calm. "What doesn't make any
sense?"

"I have never felt comfortable with Julia coming back as a
ghost," Kelly complained. "Why is she here? What's her motivation? What does she want?"

"She wants to torture me," Annie said.

"That's not enough."

Yes it is, I thought.

"Okay," Peter said, making a show of considering what
Kelly was saying. "Let's think about it. What does Julia want?"

The room was silent as everyone considered the question. I saw Julia as an extension of Melanie in this scene. She wasn't alive. Her wants were irrelevant. It was only Melanie's wants that were important. Would she be able to survive her sister's death.

Peter turned to me. "Jennifer? Is there anything you want to say here?"

I shook my head. I wanted to hear where they'd go without me.

"Okay," Peter said, "let's think about this. Julia is dead. She's probably angry that she's dead. She probably wants some sort of revenge on her sister."

"That's all from Melanie's point of view," Kelly argued. "Julia never saw it like that. She never wanted anything bad for Melanie. She loved Melanie. And, in fact, Melanie had nothing to do with her death. Julia probably would've killed herself sooner or later, whether they had that fight or not. Do you agree with that Jennifer?"

I felt like I was walking into a trap. "Yes . . ."

"So why would she want revenge?" Kelly continued. "I don't think she wants Melanie to suffer. I think she wants Melanie to live her life to the fullest."

I frowned to myself. Her comment had an ugly ring of truth to it. Had I been writing totally from the lopsided point of view of the bitter downtrodden sister instead of keeping a healthy perspective on the whole picture?

Annie spoke up. "But this scene isn't about Julia's wants or needs. Her wants and needs are over. It's about Melanie. It's Melanie fighting with the inside of her head, her guilty conscience. And it's a very theatrical way of showing that it doesn't matter what Julia wants because even though she's there— she's only there because Melanie can still imagine her."

I was glad she said that. For one thing it was nice to hear her championing Melanie for once. For another, it was totally in line with what I'd been thinking. But Kelly didn't buy it.

"I can't act that. It feels false."

I wondered if Kelly didn't like this scene because Julia takes a backseat. Out of the spotlight. Secondary. Not the main character. And she just couldn't stand that, just like Julia couldn't, just like Diana couldn't. But that was how I wanted it. After a lifetime of letting my sister be the main character in our family, I wasn't going to let her take over my play.

"So what if . . ." Peter was saying, "Julia misses her little sister and she wants to bring her with."

"Bring her with?" Kelly asked.

"She wants Melanie to get so upset, she'll feel like she doesn't deserve to live, so she'll kill herself too, and then they can be together. In a selfish but loving way, Julia wants her sister by her side."

Okay, I thought. I didn't really buy it, but at least that would give her motivation.

Kelly considered this. "You're suggesting that Julia comes here to drive her sister to suicide so she can have someone to hang out with?" She shook head. "I don't think so."

"Why not?" Peter replied.

"Because Julia is not an egomaniac!"

"Are you sure?" I couldn't resist throwing out from my seat up in the back.

That's when Kelly turned and spoke straight to me.

"The air is taken out of the play when Julia dies. It isn't dramatic anymore. The battle is over."

"What . . ." I said, sitting forward in my seat trying not to let my voice shake, "are you suggesting?"

"I'm not suggesting anything, that's not my job. I'm just telling you, as the actress who has to say the lines out loud, that it isn't—"

"I mean, here it is," I said, my voice rising above hers, "three days before we open, and you announce this major problem you have—"

"It wouldn't have been right for me to say anything until we rehearsed it. I was hoping I would be able to work through it, but I can't. And that's why I'm speaking up now."

She looked at me, making a show of exuding reasonableness. But she wasn't trying to help. She was making trouble. Just like my sister. Hogging the attention and focusing it all on herself and her needs.

I looked at Peter for a moment, wanting him to rescue me, but he started to say the wrong thing.

"Maybe," he said, "we should take a break and think about this—"

"We are not taking a break," I said, rising from my seat and coming down to the stage. "There is nothing to think about! I am not changing this scene. It has to be this way. Or else there is no final confrontation—"

"The final confrontation," she interrupted, "should be when Julia is alive! Because if they have that confrontation in the flesh it will be a lot more effective."

"It can't be when she's alive!" I said, practically screaming straight into Kelly's face. "Because it's her death. . . ! It's her death . . . ! It's her death that is the final, the final . . ." (where were the words, where was my breath?) ". . . the final worst possible most horrible most devastating thing that could happen! So how can I accomplish that if Julia is still alive?!"

Kelly looked at me—not impressed—and responded with the classic line that actors and directors love to say to writers.

"I'm not pretending to tell you how to write your play. I'm just trying to point out what's not working."

She was so cool. So self-assured. So confident. While I was there shaking and sweating like my entire existence was on the line. And I had to ask myself, Was this the same defensiveness that surfaced when Peter tried to get me to raise the stakes in the other scene? Would I wake up tomorrow and realize that she was right and I was wrong?

No. It had to be this way. Julia died and then Melanie had to face her demons.

"It's not the same," I said, trying to keep my voice steady, "to wish someone dead and then see them go on living . . . as it is to wish someone dead and then see them die."

There was a weird moment of silence.

"I am trying to dramatize Melanie's fear," I went on, "that she is responsible for the death. That by wishing it, she made it happen. I know it's not a very attractive thing, to admit to wishing someone dead. But unfortunately, it's real. And that's what this scene is about. So how can she confront that horror if Julia is still alive?"

It was mortifying. To proclaim in front of these people, barely disguised in the form of a scene in a play, that I had wished my sister dead.

But I also felt, having stated it so clearly, an incredible sense of relief. Especially since it didn't really seem to faze anyone very much.

"We all know your sister's death upset you very much," Kelly said, "but if you really want to make this a good play, you're going to have to get some perspective. You were not the most important person in your sister's life. Your sister did not kill herself because of you."

At that, she grabbed her water bottle and her black patent leather hand bag and stormed out of the room, slamming the door behind her.

Annie, Peter, Carol and I looked at each other.

"Well," Peter said with disgust, "I guess rehearsal is over for today." He headed for the office. "I might as well take care of some business."

Annie immediately went to stuff her script in her backpack. "This is fucked."

Carol took off right away. "I'm out of here."

I lingered in the lobby, not knowing what to do with myself. I was still shaking and my whole bra felt soggy with sweat, and I needed Peter to say something to me, something reassuring. So I stood outside his office and looked in the doorway. But now the publicist was bothering him about some reservations a group of NYU students had made and whether they should be comped in, and I couldn't get his attention. Or he didn't want to give it. But I felt so agitated from my outburst. Spooked. That wasn't like me. So I hovered. And finally he turned to me.

"Jennifer. I'll call you later," he said, basically dismissing me.

"Do you think she'll come around?"

"I'll have a talk with her."

"I can't believe that with this little time left, she has to storm out like that."

Peter scowled. And I didn't feel very reassured. But then he said "Actresses" in a mocking way and then he winked at me. I appreciated that wink, whether it was genuine or not. It would help get me through the night.

I hit the bathroom before leaving, and was glad to find Annie there. She stood in front of the mirror applying make-up.

"You don't usually wear makeup, do you? When you're not performing?" I asked, not wanting to immediately address the disaster rehearsal had just been.

"My agent says I have to."

"Why?"

"She says I look too plain without it."

"That's ridiculous."

I didn't wear any myself, other than lipstick. I had boxes of makeup rescued from Diana's bathroom sitting in my closet at home. Lipsticks, mascara, lotions and creams. One case had about a hundred different shades of eye shadow. I never touched any of it. I knew I never would. But I couldn't throw any of it out.

"I don't like it," Annie said, "But my agent says I should. I don't know. Maybe it's good for me. Get rid of this girl-next-door image and glam it up."

"Just to go home on the subway?"

"She wants me to get used to looking like this all the time."

"So you can feel permanently dissatisfied with your natural looks?"

"Don't you want to be an actress?"

"Right now I sure don't want to be a writer."

"Yeah. Sorry about rehearsal." Annie brushed mascara on her lashes.

"It's not your fault. You've been wonderful." I didn't want to interrupt this conversation to go pee, so I combed my hair just to have something to do.

"I just mean I'm sorry she had to walk out like that. We need to rehearse. I'm pissed off that she left."

"Yeah. And she's been so relatively low-maintenance up till now."

"Unlike me?"

"You've been working through your part. That's to be expected. And you never walked out on a rehearsal. That sucks."

"It sucks."

Annie put some raspberry colored lipstick on. I thought it looked too dark for her but didn't say so. I looked in the mirror and decided I could use a little color myself. I got out my own lipstick and put some on.

"I just hope she doesn't quit," I said.

"She won't."

"She might."

"She's not self-destructive like that," Annie insisted.

"But what if she refuses to do the scene the way it's written?" I pressed my lips together to even out the color. Suddenly I felt like my own shade was too light. Maybe I should get raspberry, like Annie.

"Kelly knows it's a great part. She's not going to fuck it up just because she has a quibble with the last scene."

"I hope you're right," I said, wondering if Annie secretly agreed with Kelly. Or maybe she thought I was a horrible person because I'd wished my sister dead. (That is, Melanie had wished *her* sister dead.)

Annie put her makeup away. At that moment I envied her for playing the part of Melanie and not actually having to be her. She could just leave the theater and go home and deal with her own problems, which certainly couldn't be as unpleasant as mine. At least I assumed. Because I didn't really know anything about her personal life.

Before leaving, she took a good look in the mirror and evaluated her makeover. "Success!" she said. "I don't recognize myself!"

I decided not to go to the tech rehearsal. It was a very tedious process, and tempers were bound to be flaring. Light cues, sound cues, lines and blocking all had to be coordinated. It involved a lot of nerve-wracking stopping and starting and was not satisfying for anyone. The actresses wouldn't even be able to work on their acting—they were just supposed to deliver their lines so the crew could work out their cues. And the fact that they still didn't have their lines memorized would make it worse. Let the chips fall as they may; there was nothing I could do at this point and seeing the chaos would only worry me.

But the following night was the dress rehearsal, and I had to see where we all stood. As I got ready to leave for the theater,

I considered calling Peter. I still felt like I needed some reassurance from him. But I didn't want to bother him. He had enough to worry about without having to take care of my nerves. Anyway, he was probably doing a million things at the theater. So I started out, but then the phone rang. I picked it up, hoping it was him. It was my mother.

"How are rehearsals going?" she asked.

"Could be better."

"Still don't want us to come?"

"Let's see how it goes."

"I'm sure it's going to be wonderful."

"Yeah, well, we'll see . . ."

She knew the play was about two sisters. She didn't know anything more than that.

"Well, good luck tonight."

"Thanks."

"I love you." My parents had taken to saying that more often since my sister died. People in my family didn't say those words, as adults at least, very often. If at all.

"I love you," I said, still awkward with the words myself. But if she was going to be saying it, I wasn't going to make myself look bad by being the one who couldn't. And, after all, I did love her. Despite the fact that she had always expected me to take care of myself, and never have any of my own problems, and always be there for Diana. Despite the fact that I knew they missed her in a horrible way and now they had to settle on just having me and I was a totally inadequate replacement. Not that they really had settled on me. Because I couldn't replace her. Even if I hadn't been so different from her. Even if I were her identical twin. Even if I wanted to.

Other than those minor issues, I had no problems with my mother.

We hung up. I felt relieved to have that conversation over with. We didn't talk much about Diana's suicide, and I suppose we were all in our own private torture chambers of guilt. But my guilt had to be different from theirs. And I felt anxious over what they would perceive of Melanie's wrath towards Julia. Maybe it would offend them. Maybe it would make them want to disown me. I'd pushed those thoughts to the back of my mind so I could write it all out, but I still didn't want them to see it. Not yet. Not until I'd seen it work in front of an audience of strangers.

And now, with the questions Kelly was raising, I really didn't want them to be there scrutinizing it.

I started out again, but the phone rang once more. This time it was Peter.

"Hi," he said, "I'm calling from the theater."

"Something wrong?"

"No. I just want to know how you're doing."

"I'm okay. Thanks."

"Don't let Kelly get to you."

"Do you think her problem," I couldn't resist asking, "do you think there's any validity to what she says?"

"No."

"I'm glad to hear that."

"I think she's totally off the mark," he added.

"Why do you think she waited so long to speak up? And why does she suddenly think she's Miss Literary Critic?"

"She wants to make trouble."

"But why?!"

"Because," he said wryly, "she's turned into Julia."

"Oh my God." A smile found its way to my face. "You're right."

"And that's exactly what we want."

After we hung up, I felt a wave of optimism. Maybe this fuss had nothing to do with how the last scene was written. And her behavior was a positive development. Something inevitable and necessary. Kelly was embodying Julia, and everything was falling into place!

I knew that I shouldn't assume this scenario was true. But in the theater, Hope Springs Eternal.

Kelly was late, no surprise, for the dress rehearsal. And when she did finally arrive after forty-five minutes, she didn't even have the grace to pretend to be flustered or apologetic. Peter looked to her for an explanation but she gave none. She just said, casually, "Oh, fuck, you know what? I forgot my costume for the first scene."

My sister, I thought, has risen from the dead.

I could see Peter tense up, but all he said was, "We're already behind schedule. Let's start."

Kelly looked at him with a vixenish smile. "Whatever you say."

Then she smiled at me. I gave her a big smile right back. Yes, this was part of her "process" of embodying Julia, which meant she was feeling quite superior to us all right then, and none of us were worth her time or effort, and if she'd just listened to her agent she would have a paying job on a soap right now. Yes sir, she was too good for us. Well too bad, I thought. That's what older sisters are for.

"Places everyone," Carol announced, "we're ready to begin!"

Unfortunately the lighting and the sound person were now missing. Carol found them out in the hallway, leisurely returning from a coffee run having gotten used to the idea that nothing was going to happen right away, and just as she was calling them in Peter came up behind her and yelled, "Get your butts in here!"

So now everyone was in a sour mood.

The houselights dimmed, the lead-in music played, the actresses took their places on stage, the music faded out and the lights came up. Peter and Carol watched from the first row. I watched from the back row. The actresses said their lines and moved around on stage. But something was, of course, wrong.

Kelly was up there saying the lines, but she wasn't acting. The performance, if you can call it that, was affectless. If anything, she reminded me of a sullen teenager who's been told she has to spend time with her nine-year-old cousin or she won't get the car Saturday night. *Okay, I'll say the lines, but I'm not going pretend like I care about them.* I squirmed in my seat. Seemed like she was taking this "embodying my sister thing" a little too far. I fleetingly wondered if this behavior could be fallout from our bedroom encounter. But I just couldn't take that thought seriously.

Peter let them go on. The point of the dress rehearsal was to give everyone a chance to run through the play without interruption. This was especially important considering they hadn't succeeded in doing that yet. So I knew he didn't want to stop them. But as the first scene came to a dismal end, he stopped them.

"Please start from the beginning again," he said. "And Kelly, could you please put some feeling into it this time?"

"I thought I was," she said.

"I think we should go on," Annie said. "I need to do it beginning to end without stopping—I need to do that."

"We are doing it again," Peter insisted. "And we will do it until Kelly starts to act. I don't care if we're here all night."

So Kelly continued with her nonperformance. Annie, with nothing to play off, gave a bad performance too. And I couldn't help but think that this play was dull. Dull, dull, dull. Talk, talk, talk. Who cared about these two people? Certainly not me.

Peter didn't stop them this time. He didn't say anything. He was probably sitting there ruminating on why he hadn't gone to Hollywood to direct movies. Maybe he was deciding to go right then and there. He was thinking about who would sublet his New York apartment. Where he could buy a cheap car. What old friends he could look up. Who would let him crash at their place until he found his own. Sure, he "loved the theater." But at least they pay you to suffer in Hollywood.

It got worse. When they finally got to the (dreaded) last scene, Annie segued into lines from the second scene by mistake and Kelly went along with her so that it was like a game of Chutes and Ladders and we all had to go back near the beginning and work our way to the end all over again. I kept waiting for Peter to stop them, but he didn't. He was probably amusing himself by debating whether to look for an apartment in Santa Monica or Studio City. Direct movies or TV. Sign with an agent or stay freelance. Carol was madly flipping through the pages of the master script trying to figure out where the hell they were, and I was considering coming out with a totally uncharacteristic shriek at the top of my lungs (with my hair standing straight up on end) when Annie finally stopped the farce.

"I'm sorry," she said. "I'm totally lost."

She looked at Peter hopelessly.

He said nothing back.

"Where do you want us to start, Peter?" Annie asked.

Still he didn't respond. Kelly stood there silently, innocently, enjoying every second of how badly this was going.

"Peter?" Annie said, now getting downright desperate. "Should we go back to the beginning of the last scene?"

Peter didn't speak for a few moments. Finally he said, "You know what?" He shrugged nonchalantly. "I'm not worried. And you know why? Because I'm not going to be sitting here tomorrow night. I'm going to be in the bar down the street having a nice cold glass of beer!" And then he stood up. From the first row riser, he loomed down on them. "But you two? You two are the ones who are going to humiliate yourselves in front of an audience full of people!"

This was not, ideally, what I wanted him to be saying. She was getting to him, and he was cracking.

"Fine," Annie said, and turned to Kelly. "Kelly? Let's just do the last scene, okay?!"

"I don't see the point. The last scene doesn't work."

"Okay," Annie said, trying to remain calm. "Let's talk this out. Tell us again what your problem is. We can figure it out."

"Since when are you the director?" Kelly said.

"You're still having trouble with being the ghost, right?" Annie persisted. "So maybe you should just forget the idea that you're a ghost. There must be some other way to approach it."

"I feel," Kelly said, "like I can't breathe right now."

She took a long drink from her water bottle, gathered her things, and started for the door.

"We can talk this out," Annie pleaded.

"I have to get out of here."

"But you can't leave!" Annie followed her to the door. "Tomorrow is opening night! We haven't even done the whole play through yet!"

"And you know what?" Kelly yelled, throwing the water bottle right past Annie's head, "I don't give a flying fuck!" The water bottle hit the wall and fell to the floor.

And she left.

And we all looked at each other.

"Jesus Christ," Carol said.

"Are you okay, Annie?" I asked.

"Yeah. Good thing her aim isn't too good. This is fucked. I need to rehearse. She can't do this!"

"She just did," Peter said.

At first, I didn't feel as panicked as I could've. Because I knew that all sorts of stupid, annoying, outrageous things happen at rehearsals, but only what happens in the performance is important. And I knew she could do this part. More than ever. I mean, she was now a living, breathing Julia. There was no reason to think she couldn't pull it off tomorrow night.

If she showed up.

What is it they say? Ninety-five percent of being successful is just showing up.

And then I realized that she actually might not show up. Because that's what my sister would've done. She would've found something to be so pissed off about, she wouldn't have shown up. After all, isn't suicide just one really big way of never showing up?

Not that I thought Kelly would commit suicide.

I just thought she might not show up.

"I'm gonna talk to her," I said.

"Jennifer, stay out of it," Peter said. "I'll call her later."

"No!" I said, "she can't do this!" And I ran after her.

I wasn't sure what I was going to say. I just knew I had to say something, and that something would have to come to me before I caught up to her. So I ran, hoping to find her at the elevator. But I didn't see her in the hall. She probably took the stairs. So I took off down the stairs too, and ran through the lobby out onto the street. There—I saw her up the block just about to turn the corner, and I ran after her. By the time I reached her by the next corner, I was huffing (really had to join a gym) and puffing.

"Kelly! Stop! Kelly!"

"Not interested," she said, and didn't stop walking.

"We have to talk."

"I have a headache. I'm going home."

"Stop walking and listen to me!" I yelled.

She stopped walking.

"What is it?"

We were standing in front of a sofabed store with an incredibly garish display of a living room set done in tiger skin and brown leather. People were walking by not really noticing us, but it wasn't exactly private.

"Can we go somewhere a little less public?"

"I'd like to get home, Jennifer. If you have anything to say just get it out."

She looked at me and waited.

"I don't want you to perform my play," I heard myself say, "if you can't do the ending the way I wrote it."

"I can do your ending," she said. "I just don't think it's any good."

"You're imposing your vision onto mine. It's not right."

"Are you firing me?"

"I'm telling you to do your job. Say the words I wrote."

"I'll say your words," she said. "But I don't believe in them."

"That's not good enough."

A crowded bus pulled up to the curb.

"For the audience or for you?"

"For me!" The back doors of the bus opened, and people started pouring out.

"Well get over it, Melanie!" (We both heard her make the slip, but she didn't bother to correct it.) "Because it doesn't matter if I think your play gives a fair and accurate portrayal of your relationship with your sister. The play has to stand on its own. For all of us who don't know anything about you and your fucked-up childhood."

A woman passing by gave me a look.

"I'm not the one bringing my own personal garbage into this situation."

"Oh, really?"

"The last scene of the play isn't the problem here. The real problem is the fact that you're jealous."

"Of?"

"The fact that Peter wants me and not you!"

Right then, I wouldn't have been surprised if she morphed into a fifteen-foot-tall fire-breathing dragon, picked me up with her fangs and threw me across the street into the window of the Banana Republic. But she didn't. She just looked at me for a moment with surprise, and then a smile gradually blossomed on her face.

"Don't worry," she said. "I'll do your little play the way you want. Now just run along home and get a good night's sleep. Tomorrow's a big day for you."

With that, she headed on up the street.

"My 'little' play."

I hated her right then.

But not as much as I would hate her later.

Chapter
11

The next morning I was in such a mental state I couldn't stand the idea of being alone. Even though it was only eleven in the morning, I wandered over to the theater hoping someone would be hanging around. It was a weekday, and it was odd passing through midtown, seeing everyone going about their business like a regular day. A regular day of rushing around to their jobs, rushing to buy things, rushing with such a great sense of purpose. I walked through Macy's just for the hell of it and walked past the men's shirts and ties and the cases of watches and jewelry and makeup and purses and got sprayed with perfume and came out the other end back onto the street. The world of commerce was chugging along just fine despite the fact that this was opening night for my play.

When I got down to the theater Carol was there. I was happy to see her. She was sweeping the stage, lucky her, with a job, with a purpose!

"Hi Carol!"

"So, the big day has finally arrived."

"Is there anything I can do?"

"You could make sure there's toilet paper in the bathroom."

"Okay. Where do you keep it?"

"I'm just kidding. That's not the playwright's job."

"I don't care."

"You are desperate, aren't you."

"Anything to keep me busy."

"You know what? Peter's out getting the programs from the printer. When he comes back, you can help fold."

"That sounds perfect. How is his mood?"

"He's in a great mood."

"He is?" I went up on stage and looked down on the empty seats.

"Came in this morning happy as a clam."

"Are clams really happy?" I asked, sitting down on Melanie's bed.

"What?"

"How do they know that clams are really happy?" I lay back on the bed and looked at the lights clamped onto pipes running across the ceiling. It would not be good to have one of those fall on your head. "I mean 'clamming up' isn't really a happy thing."

"He did have some interesting news. There was a message this morning on the answering machine. Rocco Shorenstein made a reservation."

I sat straight up. "You're kidding." He was a big Broadway producer. Too big for us, really. "Why?" I asked.

"Why what?"

"Why would he be coming to this two-character drama? He does musicals. British imports. Star vehicles."

"Beats me."

"Wow. Well. That puts a nice little extra pressure on everyone, doesn't it."

"Sort of makes you wish we'd gotten through the whole thing once without stopping."

"Yep."

And if Kelly hadn't gone off on her little hissy fit, we'd be in much better shape. Oh man oh man oh man. Rocco Shorenstein was coming to see my play.

"I don't know if I should hope he comes or not," I said, getting the dustpan and holding it out for her.

"Don't worry. Half the time they make a reservation they don't show up." She swept a pile of dirt into the dustpan.

"Or they just send in an assistant who writes up a report."

"And it gets filed away."

"And that," I said, dumping the dirt into the garbage pail, "is that."

Just then Peter came bounding in, all cheerful and light.

"Good morning! Did you hear the great news?"

"Good morning, yes I did."

"Rocco Shorenstein. Isn't it great?"

"How did you pull this off?"

"I know someone who works in his office. Been trying to get him to come to my stuff for years. You see? Persistence pays."

"Does he have to come opening night? I mean, it sure would be better if he could wait till they have a chance to, you know—"

Carol finished for me. "Do it once without stopping."

"You can't control the world of theater," Peter said. "Too many competing egos. Just have to go with the flow. Who'd like to fold some programs?"

"I'd love to," I said. "It will help calm my nerves."

"Relax, you have nothing to worry about."

"Other than the play being a disaster," I said, taking a stack of the glossy pages.

"You're being negative again, Jennifer."

"Just working my magic."

"You don't have to work any magic. Everything is going to come together tonight."

"How can you believe that?"

"I just do. I have every confidence that it's going to be great tonight."

"But what about Kelly?"

"Had a long talk with her last night. Everything is cool."

"She's okay about the last scene?"

"Uh huh."

"What did you say to her?"

"I said what I had to say. The crisis has passed."

"Huh. That's good, I guess."

We started in on the programs, not speaking for the moment. I didn't read them. Seeing my name in print made me anxious. But folding them in neat halves and then smoothing them down flat had a very placating effect. I didn't want them to run out.

The phone rang and Carol went to get it. "Hi Annie. Yeah, he's here, hold on."

Peter took the phone.

"Hi Annie, what's up? Uh huh. Uh huh. Uh huh. Okay. Well. That's fine. It doesn't sound like it should be a problem. Right. Right. Right. Okay. Fine. Good. Congratulations. See you later." He hung up.

"What now?" I asked.

"Annie got a job."

"A job?"

"A job."

"What do you mean?"

"One line on *Law and Order*."

"When?"

"Today."

"Today?

"Today. One line. They're paying her six hundred fifty-five dollars. She felt she had to grab it."

I stood up. "I'll pay her six hundred fifty-five *not* to do it!"

"Come on," Peter said. "She can't turn it down. It's a good credit. And it won't be a problem. They've been shooting since seven this morning. And they've told her she'll be done well before five."

"But these things can go overtime."

"Don't worry. They hate overtime because they have to pay everyone up the wazoo."

"But today it will go overtime! Today her one line will be in the last scene they shoot and something will go wrong so they have to stay late because God knows my play is opening tonight!"

"Forget about it! She'll be here with plenty of time to spare."

"I think I'm getting a headache."

"You know what? You should go home and sleep off the day. You're just going to be a wreck till the first line is spoken."

"As if I could sleep."

"Take two Tylenol, you'll sleep."

I groaned. I didn't like the idea of being with myself all day. Maybe getting comatose was the answer. I handed Carol my folded programs.

"Relax," she said, "even if it is a total disaster . . . in the end it won't matter to anyone but you."

I walked back home and actually did intend on taking both my homeopathic sleep-aid and two Tylenol, but when I got inside I saw a message blinking on my machine.

"Jennifer. Darling." It was Kelly. "It's around noon and I happen to be in midtown so I was wondering if you'd like to get together for lunch. I felt so badly about yesterday, and was hoping we could clear things up before the performance tonight. Because I'm really not jealous, and the situation is not what you think. Call me on my cell, okay?"

Clear everything up? She wasn't jealous? What did she

mean? I told myself not to call her, not to give in to the temptation. It wasn't worth the risk of making things worse. I should just take my nap, and see her later at the theater. I shouldn't even speak to her again until after the performance.

But then it occurred to me. Maybe her behavior was because of the fact that I didn't respond that night she tried to seduce me. After all, wasn't there a real attraction between the two of us? And even though she knew I was struggling with my own inhibitions, that didn't mean she wouldn't also take it personally. But I had never acknowledged that possibility to her or to me because I was more comfortable centering our problems around Peter.

Or maybe that's not what she meant at all.

I listened to the message again. *"Because I'm really not jealous, and the situation is not what you think."*

Maybe I was right. Maybe she wasn't feeling jealous, she was feeling rejected. And not by Peter, but by me. And all her big talk about being attracted to Peter had been a cover for her attraction to me. After all, I was the one she'd gotten into her bed, not him.

Now I was dying of curiosity to know if this was the truth. But I really didn't trust her. Or myself. It would be smarter to leave things alone until after they had a performance under their belt.

Though she did want to speak to me. And if she was feeling rejected, it would hurt her feelings not to call . . .

I looked at the container of Tylenol. I looked at the phone. Tylenol? Phone? Tylenol? Phone? I couldn't resist. I picked up the phone and dialed.

We met at Amelia's, an odd kind of cool and trendy restaurant tucked away in the west 50s between Tenth and Eleventh Avenue near a recycling center for aluminum cans that employed a lot of homeless people. The block was made up of a row of old brownstones that were so run-down they looked abandoned, but there were still people actually living in them. And then there was the pretty little yellow-trimmed facade of Amelia's in the only renovated brownstone on the block.

On the weekends there was always a line of people waiting for a table. But since this was a Wednesday, we had no problem getting seated right away.

We were shown to a table in the backyard. That was what was so great about this place. It was right in the middle of Hell's Kitchen New York City and you go to the backyard and you think you're in the country. Well, not exactly, but you can pretend. Sort of. Well . . . Let's just say that there were some trees there. And tables under the trees. Not that I care that much about trees. But it was nice to sit among them occasionally. And it was sunny and there were trails of ants on the ground. You don't get trails of ants on the ground too much in New York City, so there's something kind of neat about it in a countryesque sort of way. You don't see many ants in New York City, come to think of it. Come to think of it, maybe I'm imagining the ants.

In any case, it was nice.

All you had to do was block out the fact that in the buildings on all sides of you were people living off welfare who would die to have your eggs benedict.

But they were behind a tall wood fence through which you couldn't see. So it was sort of like they didn't exist. Sort of.

We sat down at a small round table. The stressed-out waitresses rushed back and forth. There were too many people trying to enjoy this bucolic setting and not enough people to serve them. Our waitress, an angry looking woman with black hair cut in a page boy style, black lipstick, black sleeveless shirt and black capris (for some reason I have a vivid memory of her) brought a crock of butter and a little loaf of fresh baked white bread to the table. Kelly started in on the bread right away. She loved bread and butter. And then we ordered the poached eggs with hollandaise sauce, which of course has a ton more of butter.

"So, I said. "Peter told me he talked with you about the play last night."

"Oh, yes. Everything is fine."

"Good."

I considered telling her about Rocco Shorenstein. But sometimes it's best not to tell an actor that someone important is going to be in the audience. It adds that extra tension they just don't need. So I didn't mention it.

But I felt too nervous to bring the conversation around to her and me.

So I offered up the other big news.

"Annie got a day's work on *Law and Order.*"

"Did she? Good for her."

"Today."

"Today?"

"But everyone assures me they'll be done by five."

"A speaking part?"

"One line."

"How'd she get it?"

"I think she knows the gaffer."

"Oh, right, she mentioned that. Good for her."

The waitress brought the food. I decided it would be nice not to talk about anything having to do with theater, television or movies. And we savored those eggs. I savor them now in my memory—each precious little bite of egg, with just the right ratio of yolk and white, dipped in that evil, tasty buttery lemony sauce, and washed down with good strong coffee with half-and-half.

Yes, it was a beautiful, sunny day. Nothing could be more perfect. The world was a wonderful place.

"So I'm sorry," I found myself apologizing, "if I was out of line yesterday."

"Don't be ridiculous," she said, "you're nervous about your play."

"Yeah. It's silly when all this other stuff starts interfering."

"Don't worry about it."

"Because I'd hate to think I upset you."

"Not at all."

"Good. Because you said something in your message about the situation not being what I thought."

"Yes. I decided I should be straightforward with you about this. Because I care about you, Jennifer. I really do. And I know I can be difficult. And I don't want you to think I'm being a bitch."

"So . . . I'm confused about whatever it is you're being straightforward about."

"Right. Sorry. It's sort of hard to tell you this."

She hesitated, so I thought I'd help her out. "Does it have something to do with that night?"

"That night?"

"When I stayed over at your apartment. And you . . ."

I couldn't say it.

"And I what?"

"You know."

"Made you spaghetti?"

"Tried to have sex with me. And I turned you down."

"What are you saying exactly?"

"You haven't exactly been the same to me since."

She laughed a little. "Sex doesn't have to be some big emotional event, honey. It can just be two people having a good time together."

"And I couldn't have a good time with you."

"You can't have a good time with anyone. That's your problem. And it's about time you realized that the world isn't going to wait around forever for you to realize you're as horny as the rest of us."

Horny. I hate that word. Makes me think of a rhinoceros horn protruding out of a man's crotch.

"So what is it you wanted to tell me?"

"Peter and I made love last night."

I hate food that has sun on it. Sweating food. Food that sweats grease. That's why I hate picnics. I always lose my appetite at picnics, especially barbecues. I also hate touching people in the heat. I don't know how people have sex in the heat. In fact, I don't know how people from warm climates have managed to reproduce.

"Really," I said. "How was it?"

"Delicious."

"That's nice."

I looked down at my plate. The egg yolk looked back at me. Mocking me. For thinking that I was the center of the world. Hah! Forget it. As usual, I was the onlooker. The outsider. And I had no one to blame but myself. Peter had wanted me, and I had practically pushed him out of my bed and into hers. So I had no right to feel jealous. Or possessive. Or any of those things.

"You don't mind, do you?" she said. "I mean, it doesn't really matter, because you were never really into him, right?"

"Right."

"Good. I'm relieved. Because I didn't want to upset you."

"I'm happy for you."

"Well," she said, "I certainly enjoyed it. God knows I was overdue for a good fuck."

Well. I certainly had no appetite at this point. But I had to eat, for show, so I made myself, which is tragic when you think of the calories involved.

So I took a bite.

Chewed.

Swallowed.

A waitress set down two big heavy plates of waffles on the table next to us. I wondered how those people would consume those gigantic things. Puddles of greasy butter melted into the glistening maple syrup. A fly flitted around the dish. Disgusting. He actually slept with her. How could he do that? After everything he'd said about not being attracted to her.

I flashed onto what he told me that morning. "I said what I had to say." Maybe what he really meant was he did what he had to do.

"Did you sleep with Peter," I asked, "before or after you promised him you weren't going to fuck up my play?"

"Believe me. No bargain was struck. He was, like the slogan they use for those welfare people who clean the streets, READY WILLING and ABLE."

"Well. Aren't you into the social services."

"Are you jealous?"

I looked at her. Took a sip of coffee. "I told you. I'm not interested in him like that."

"But maybe you're interested in me. Not that it makes any difference who you're interested in, because you're too scared to do anything about it."

If I had just taken those two Tylenol and my homeopathic sleep-aid and drifted off into some nice, soothing sleep, I could've gone through the day in blissful ignorance.

But instead I had a throbbing headache, and I really did need some Tylenol, but I didn't have any on me. "You know what? I think I should go."

"I'll go with you. I should hit the gym and take a nice bubble bath so I'll be all fresh for tonight."

So I let Kelly walk me back to my apartment. One thing was for sure. She was in a good mood now. All of her bad mood from the past week had vanished.

"Oh, by the way," she said, "did you know? Rocco Shorenstein is coming to tonight's performance. Isn't that amazing?"

"Yeah. I know." So much for not telling her so she wouldn't be nervous. Obviously Peter had called her that morning and told her, and they'd probably celebrated with some hot phone sex. "It's too bad," I added bitterly, "we've never gone through the whole play once without stopping." Not that she had a guilty conscience.

"Don't worry. It will give us that much more energy because we're all going to be so psyched. It's going to be great, you'll see."

"Uh huh."

"Anyway, got to run," she said, and kissed me on the cheek and left. Maybe to get in another quick one with Peter.

I walked up the stairs to my apartment and took those two Tylenol as soon as I walked in the door. Then I lay down in bed and congratulated myself. This was what I had wanted, right? To keep my actress happy. Well, she was happy. Happy as a clam.

Added bonus—it was at my expense.

So everything was in place for opening night.

I pulled my covers up around me and tried to relax into a deep sleep.

But I couldn't relax. My eyes kept popping open as if there were springs on my lids. And my body. It was so tense. My back, my jaw, my shoulders, my legs. I couldn't relax. Even with the help of the Tylenol . . . even focusing on every part of my body and trying every zen, yoga relaxation technique I knew, I couldn't do it. I had to get up.

So I got up. But what to do?

I stood in the middle of the room.

Looked around my room.

Lamp. Books. Messy desk. Swivel chair. Computer. Bureau with clothes piled on top of it because they didn't fit in the

drawers. Stuffed animals from childhood, old box of choco-
lates sent from my mother last Valentine's day with a few stale
uneaten cream-filled ones left in the box that I couldn't bring
myself to throw out. I went to the mirror. Looked at myself.
That took about five seconds. Still sixty seconds times sixty
minutes times seven hours left until "curtain" (there wasn't
actually a curtain) and I had to spend it all with my own miserable self.

I decided the only thing to do was take a walk. That's something Manhattan is always good for, especially if the weather is
good. I plotted a route in my mind, a big circle—walk uptown
on Columbus Avenue, through Central Park to the East Side,
come back down Fifth Avenue, go by the Plaza and Tiffanys
and Saks and the Main Library and then, maybe on 34th
Street or 23rd Street I could just head into a movie theater and
see anything, anything at all, and then head West to the theater. That's what I was going to do.

I put on my favorite pair of black rayon pants and my lilac
silk knit top (on sale at Century 21 for seventy percent off) in
case I didn't make it back to my apartment before getting to
the theater for the performance. Hopefully I wouldn't work
up a sweat on my walk. Wearing the silk was risky. If my arm
pits did perspire, I figured I'd just have to buy a top somewhere later. If worse came to worst, there was bound to be a
Gap.

And so I flew up the streets in a sort of trance. Aimless except for my route. I didn't even want to think. I didn't like any
of my thoughts. He slept with her, he slept with her, he slept
with her. And I had practically engineered the whole thing. So
I had no right to be jealous. But that didn't mean he had to go
along with it. Didn't he know I didn't mean it? Why didn't he
give me another chance? So quickly, he gave up on me. Maybe
he was right to. Maybe I would've done the exact same thing
the second time around. Or maybe, the truth was, he didn't

care about me. But she intimidated him, and so he'd settled on me. Or maybe he'd just felt sorry for me—could tell I was attracted to him, and kissed me as a favor, but it was her he wanted all along. "I never get involved with flighty actresses," he had said. Yeah, right. Well if he was going to hurt me, then I would hurt him. I would hurt him back! I didn't know how, but I would find a way. Except . . . I didn't want to hurt him. So I tried not to think, just to move. I was on automatic. Whizzing down the streets. Lucky not to get hit by a car.

I made my way up Columbus past clothing stores and restaurants, over on 86th Street to the park, wound my way around the bottom of the reservoir staying out of the way of joggers and dog walkers, and came out of the park on Fifth Avenue near the Metropolitan Museum. Considered going inside, but the idea of looking at art and mummies seemed totally beside the point. So I kept going down Fifth, zigzagged over to Madison, down past more clothing shops and restaurants then farther east to Park Avenue past towering old prewar apartment buildings with bored doormen standing guard. Then I made my way farther east to Lexington Avenue past Hunter College and Bloomingdales, considered going in, but perfume and clothing seemed beside the point. Veered back towards Central Park and Fifth Avenue past Bergdorf's, Tiffany's, Rockefeller Center and Saks, past 42nd Street and the Main Library and Lord & Taylor and then, when I hit 34th Street, I went farther east to a movie theater and bought a ticket to a Bruce Willis movie.

Not because I wanted to see it, but because it was there.

I sat through the movie barely listening to the plot. At one point I just got up, not because it was over, not because I needed to go to the bathroom or buy popcorn. The thought just occurred to me to stand up and start walking again, so I did. (Plus the movie wasn't any good.) So I left and walked some more. And went in and out of a stationery store and a deli and a flower shop.

Flowers.

Traditional to bring flowers to the actresses on opening night. Well, maybe for Annie, but was she even going to bother to make it tonight? And forget Kelly. Peter could buy her fucking flowers. So I continued on to the theater.

It was a little past seven o'clock. The actors had been called for seven. They would be in the dressing room getting ready. I didn't want to have to face Kelly (or Peter) but there was no way around it and I didn't know where else to go. So, after hesitating a moment in front of the building, I went in through the glass doors and the marble lobby and into the elevator.

As soon as the doors of the elevator opened up to the lobby of the theater, I was back in the world.

Carol was there with Beth, an NYU acting student/intern helping out with the box office. She was showing Beth how to deal with the cash drawer and the reservation list.

"Hi you guys," I said.

Carol looked up. "Hi, how are ya?"

"Fine."

"Nervous?"

There's one thing I always feel when I go to watch my own plays. And that is the supreme relief that I am not an actress. No matter how badly it goes, at least I don't have to humiliate myself in front of all those people. Just sit in the last row, or the lobby, or the lighting booth, or the dressing room back-stage and let it happen. No matter how nervous I am, I get comfort from that.

And so I gave her my standard response. "I'm just glad I'm not an actress and I don't have to go up on stage."

Beth said, "Isn't it hard watching other people saying your lines?"

"I'm grateful to them for doing it so I don't have to."

"It would drive me crazy," she said. "But don't worry," she added with a smile. "I'm sure they're going to do a great job and your play is going to be a big success."

I knew that Beth, who was cute in a chipmunk sort of way, meant well. But she was really annoying me with her positive outlook.

"Peter wants to talk with you," Carol mentioned in her dependably morose voice. "He's in the office."

"Okay." As I went to him, I allowed myself an indulgence of hopefulness. Maybe he was going to confess his transgressions and beg my forgiveness. He gave in to her in a moment of weakness. She seduced him. He was feeling vulnerable. Rejected by me. Regretted it as soon as it happened. Could I forgive him? Would I?

Never! Or not until later that night, at least.

I knocked on the door of the office and Peter called me in. He was eating a sandwich with avocado and sprouts in it. I hated interrupting his eating. "Hi," I said. You slept with her, I thought.

"Hi."

I was hoping he would have a guilty look on his face, but it was more like distress. "Annie called," he said. "They haven't gotten to her scene yet."

"You're kidding."

"It looks like she may not make it."

I hate the theater. Why did I ever think I liked it? Because of Rising Stars and some fun high school and college productions, sure, but what ever possessed me to think I could make some kind of career out of it? Had to be out of my mind.

"If she doesn't get here soon," he continued, "I'd say we have two options."

I sank into a chair. He took a bite of sandwich. A piece of avocado hung for a moment out of his mouth. He realized it was there and wiped it off with the back of his hand. "We can either cancel the performance. Which would be a real bummer because we have reservations for a good size house."

Which was a miracle in itself.

Typical.

Spend two years writing the play. Find someone to produce it, direct it, rehearse it, build a set, lug an iron radiator from the flea market, bring in an audience that includes, against all odds, a potential investor with Broadway credits and opening night comes and you don't have your leading lady because she gets one line on *Law and Order.* That's theater in a nutshell.

"Or?" I said.

I was curious to hear what he was going to say. To me there was no alternative to cancelling. We had no understudy. What else could we do?

"You go on."

"Very funny."

"I'm dead serious."

"Playwrights do not step in for actors."

"They do if we need them to."

"I don't know the lines."

"You can do it script in hand."

"No."

"Come on. I'll go out there before we start. Make an announcement. Explain the situation."

"Forget it."

"The audience will love it—they'll be on your side!"

"I cannot go up in front of an audience. There's no way! And apart from the fact that the idea of it scares me to death, I can't act!"

"You don't have to act. Just say the lines."

"You're crazy."

"Say the lines loudly and clearly. Just so the people can hear them. And let Kelly do the rest."

"Peter! You're suffering some kind of delusion here, like we're in the middle of some hackneyed storyline where the understudy goes on for the lead and does some incredible tap dance routine and becomes a big star. But I am not an actress, I'm a writer. And everyone knows we hate going up in front of people and I'm not going to do it!"

"I am not trying to turn you into a star. I am trying to turn a bad situation into an adequate one."

"I have an idea. Ask Beth to do it. Problem solved."

"Beth?"

"She's doing box office. She's an actress from NYU."

"She doesn't know the play. She doesn't know the character."

"You said read the lines, don't act."

"Yeah but she's an actress, she'll try to act and she'll do it all wrong."

"Then let Carol do it. She knows the play backwards and forwards."

"We need Carol to run the show. Face it, Jennifer." And then he laughed in this maniacal sort of way. "You're perfect for the part."

I looked at him, not laughing, not even smiling. "I cannot go out there on that stage."

His smile quickly disappeared. "We've all worked our asses off to make this evening happen. Don't let a little stage fright make it all for nothing. Rise to the occasion."

"Rise to the occasion? You certainly rose to the occasion last night with Kelly, didn't you!"

That caught him off guard. I was a bit surprised myself, that I let that slip out. He was flummoxed, for the moment, so I pressed on.

"Peter. Believe me. It won't work. We'll ask Beth. She'll be happy to do it. And I'll do box office. I love doing box office. To be quite honest, I'm starting to believe that the only way I want to be involved in the theater from now on is by doing box office."

He looked harshly at me. "Then you're a coward," he said.

I felt some relief. I was more than willing to be a coward as long as it meant I didn't have to go on stage.

"I'm sorry," I said. "If I'm letting you down."

And sorry, I thought, that you let me down.

And I left the office.

And I passed through the lobby, where people were starting to accumulate, and escaped into the still-empty theater and took my seat in the back row.

So that's how it would work out. He would ask Beth. And she would be thrilled. And my play would be ruined. But that was okay, because there were still fifteen more performances, and who cared if Rocco Shorenstein was in the audience. Even if he did show up, which he wouldn't, he'd never do anything for me because they never do. The important thing was that I didn't have to go out there and make a fool out of myself.

I congratulated my sister. She was probably watching all of this with amusement. Getting her revenge.

Carol poked her head in. "We're going to open the house now," she said to me.

"Okay."

I got up and headed backstage. Kelly would be there, but I didn't know where else to go. So I slipped through the break in the curtain. And there she was, sitting at the makeup table putting on eyeliner.

"You'd better hurry up and get ready," she said.

She already wore the black leather miniskirt and red halter (from her own wardrobe) she wears in the first scene.

"I told him to use Beth."

She put down the eyeliner and turned around. "That little idiot at the box office? Are you insane?"

"Why not?"

"She'll ruin your play."

"As if I would do any better."

"I don't believe this. Where's your copy of the script?"

"I don't have it."

"Then use mine."

"I am not going out there."

"Jennifer. Rocco Shorenstein is going to be here."

"Maybe."

"Not maybe. Probably. And you are not going to ruin this for me."

Ruin this for her? What a delightful idea. I looked at her innocently. "Why shouldn't I?"

"Oh. I get it. You want to get back at me because of Peter. And you're willing to sacrifice your play to do it."

"Why not? The last scene isn't any good anyway."

She stepped towards me. For a second I thought she was going to slap me on the cheek like Rhett Butler slaps Scarlett in *Gone With the Wind*.

"If you don't go out there and say your goddamned words that you wrote because you wanted, more than anything, for an audience to hear what you have to say, then you belong at home watching TV along with the rest of the country. You don't belong in the theater."

We looked at each other. My right eye twitched. Neither of my eyes, to my knowledge, had ever twitched before.

"But . . ." I said feebly, "I can't."

"Yes you can."

"No. I can't. Even if I wanted to go out there . . ."

"What?"

"It's impossible."

"Why?"

"Because I can't do it."

"Because . . . ?"

"Because . . ." I thought of telling Kelly I had my period. And it was my first day, so the flow was really heavy and the bloating and cramping was really bad. But for once I didn't have my period on an important day. Then my petrified eyes landed on the pair of blue jeans Annie wears in the first scene. "The costumes. I'll never fit into them. Annie wears like a size four."

"Forget the costumes. People can imagine the clothes. It doesn't matter."

"So you're saying go out there just like this?"

She looked me up and down, unimpressed. "It will do." She handed me her script. "Brush your hair and put on some lipstick. I'll tell Peter."

"But—"

She left. And that's when I realized . . . I was going to do it. I was actually going to do it.

I started to shake. I'm not talking tremble. I'm talking shake, like naked in a blizzard. Even my jaw shook, violently, like I'd lost motor control. I took deep breaths in and out but it didn't do a bit of good. I brushed my hair. Clumsily. Fingers didn't work right. Tried to put on lipstick but couldn't hold my hand still enough to do it, couldn't find the strength to apply enough pressure to put it on.

Oh God. This was a big mistake.

I went to the curtain, opened it an inch and looked through. A surprising number of people were starting to arrive. I had an urge to scream from behind the curtain: *Don't you people have anything better to do than come here on this beautiful evening and sit in this hot stuffy theater and watch my depressing play?!*

I went back to the dressing room and sat down. Opened Kelly's script as if I was seeing my play for the first time. The pages were wrinkled and ragged, with all her lines highlighted in fat fluorescent yellow. I could barely see my own lines between them.

She came back. "He's going to make an announcement and explain the situation and then we'll go on."

"What about the blocking?"

"You've seen it a million times, Jennifer, it will come to you."

"No. I mean, I don't think I can move."

"What?"

"My limbs are frozen."

"Listen. All actors feel nervous just before they're about to go out. It'll go away as soon as you start speaking your lines."

"No it won't."

"It will. I mean, my God. People are not going to be judging your performance."

"Yes they will. People always judge, you know that. They can't help themselves."

"But they're not expecting a performance from you. And you shouldn't expect that from yourself. Just forget about the audience. It's you and me out there. You and me talking. All you have to do is let them listen to you."

"I don't want them to listen to me."

"That's what you want more than anything. That's why you wrote this play!"

Carol stuck her head in. "Peter is going to make his announcement and start the show, so you better be ready."

Chapter

12

Kelly and I stood in the wing, where we could see Peter facing the audience. Little dots of dust, illuminated by the bright lights, floated in the air around him.

"Good evening Ladies and Gentlemen, and welcome to The Renegade Theater. I'm Peter Heller, and I have a treat for all of you tonight. As you may or may not know, this production is an Equity Showcase, and the code for this type of performance means that our actors are performing gratis. It also means that if one of them gets a paying acting job, she has the option of taking that job even if it conflicts with the performance schedule. Well, one of our two leading ladies got a one-day gig on *Law and Order*, and the shoot went overtime."

The audience reacted with a groan.

"I'm told she only has one line, and that line is, 'How much am I going to get paid?'"

People laughed. Ha ha.

"But we didn't want to cancel the show tonight. So our esteemed playwright has graciously agreed to read the part of Melanie for us tonight."

There was a round of surprised mumblings in the audience and some applause. A wave of acid flooded my stomach.

"She will have the script in hand. And she's a little nervous. But I know you'll all be very supportive of her. I hope you all enjoy tonight's performance of *Til Death Do Us Part* by Jennifer Ward."

Everyone applauded enthusiastically. Yes, I thought, they're going to eat this up. This was better than any play. This was like Reality TV. Watch the playwright humiliate herself on stage.

The lights went down.

I followed Kelly out onto the stage like a child who tags after her mother in a crowded department store. Don't lose me! If I was short enough, I would've clutched the hem of her skirt. I became horribly conscious of a hush that came over the audience, our visitors, our guests who had invaded our safe little space and were now expecting to be entertained. *Don't listen to me,* I wanted to scream. *I have nothing to say!*

I found my way to my place upstage. It was hot under the lights. The glare made me squint. I gripped my script. Kelly stood next to me. She had the first line.

Julia: *"So how do you like your new apartment?"*

My line. My line. I knew my line without needing to look into my script. The line was in my head. But all these people were looking at me. Waiting for me. Maybe even Rocco, who had to be that fat man sitting in the front row.

All I had to do was say my line. Say it out loud. Say it! I cleared my throat. My voice came out—small and barely audible.

Melanie: *"It's small."*

I looked at Kelly. She looked at me with impatience, a lot like Diana would've done.

"No view," I continued. *"The ceiling is low. It never gets a drop*

of sun. And I've already stepped on two cockroaches. It's the epitome of Hell's Kitchen—"

Julia: *"Glamour!"*

Melanie: *"I was going to say grunge. I never thought I'd feel lucky to live in a place with bars on the windows."*

Julia: *"That's the good kind that you can slide open if there's a fire. An accessory every young lady should have."*

Melanie: *"Great."*

I relaxed on that word. I was used to being sarcastic. And it was reassuring that I could hear my own voice in Melanie's lines. But I had to project. I made myself stand up straight while Kelly gave her line.

Julia: *"Not to mention, it keeps the wolves at bay. On the fifth floor there's always the danger of someone breaking in from the roof."*

I took a big breath and tried to speak from my stomach. Isn't that what actresses do? Not from the throat but from the stomach?

Melanie: *"You aren't mad at me, are you? Because I'm not staying with you?"*

This was worse. I still sounded stiff—just louder.

Julia: *"Of course not. You need your own place. It's Mom and Dad who wanted you to keep an eye on me."*

Melanie: *"You're the one who's going to have to keep an eye on me. This city intimidates me, and I don't know a soul."*

That line came out better. I sounded halfway natural.

Julia: *"Don't worry. Manhattan is the easiest place in the world to meet people. And no matter how many enemies you make, there's always a fresh supply of unsuspecting people to take their place."*

The audience laughed. That relaxed me more. I started to see how I could get into this. It was fun to have Kelly speak my lines back to me. No wonder they called them plays. We were playing!

Melanie: *"I certainly feel like it's going to make me face all my fears."*

Julia: *"No better place on earth to face your fears than New York City."*

By the time we came to the yelling out the window section, I was so into it, I had to stop myself from overacting.

Julia: *"You have to think positively if you want to get anywhere in this world. Now I want you to repeat after me."*

Kelly slid open the gate, raised the window and stuck her head out.

Julia: *"I am ambitious!"*

Melanie: *"No."*

Julia: *"Say it! Go ahead."*

Melanie: *"This is idiotic."*

Julia: (yelling) *"I am ambitious!"*

I went to the window. Since I'd already done this in real life in her apartment, it didn't seem so alarming. I had to remind myself to hold back.

Melanie: *"I am ambitious."*

Julia: (yelling) *"And I deserve to succeed!"*

Melanie: *"Do I have to?"*

Julia: (yelling) *"I deserve to succeed!"*

Melanie: *"I deserve to succeed. I suppose."*

The audience laughed. I felt grateful. They were letting me (and Melanie) know they were with me (and her).

We continued on to the end of the scene and the lights faded out. Kelly quickly changed her clothes. In what seemed like no time, we were back out on stage. A year has passed. Melanie is engaged to be married. And she's wracked with guilt. I was doing fine until we got about midway through. And then I started to get uncomfortable.

Melanie: *"We never talked about this, all these years, but . . . do you remember the day you tried to kill yourself?"*

Julia: *"Of course."*

Melanie: *"I felt sure I had done something wrong. Like I was responsible, somehow, for what happened."*

Julia: *"That's ridiculous."*

Melanie: *"You want to know something weird?"*

Julia: *"Sure."*

I hesitated. Melanie had a monologue. I felt naked, because it was drawn so much from my own life, and annoyed. Why couldn't I fictionalize more? It was too late now. I made myself go on.

Melanie: *"The day you did it, was the first day I got my period. I was sort of freaked out, because I'd stained the crotch of my pants and I was horrified that maybe someone at school had seen something. And I went straight home and found Mom on the floor of the bathroom. Cleaning blood off the floor. Sobbing on the floor. And she told me about you. And it was horrible. And . . . I couldn't tell her."*

Julia: *"Why not?"*

Melanie: *"It suddenly didn't seem very important."*

Julia: *"Or maybe you didn't want her to know."*

Melanie: *"That I'd gotten my period?"*

Julia: *"That you'd become a woman. Like me."*

Kelly and I looked at each other. I wondered if the audience was following everything I was trying to set up. I felt worried about what was coming. But I was also looking forward to it. Stop thinking, I told myself. Stay in the moment.

Melanie: *"I know this is difficult for you."*

Julia: *"It's not. I'm glad we're talking about this. We should've done this a long time ago."*

Melanie: *"No, I mean the fact that I'm getting married."*

Julia: *"I'm glad you're getting married, Melanie. I want you to be happy."*

Melanie: *"But it will be hard for you to go out there in front of everyone and have to smile . . ."*

Julia: (Raising her voice) *"Oh, please. I would never want to marry George, or someone even vaguely like George!"*

Melanie: *"But you hate it, don't you. You hate the fact that I'm the one who's getting married first!"*

I looked at Kelly and felt my moment of triumph. She took her hairbrush and threw it at my head. I jumped aside when it almost hit me.

Then she came to sit down next to me on the bed, apologized, smoothed my hair, rubbed my back. It felt horrible. Just like I used to feel with my sister. That paralyzing mixture of guilt and anger. Hating her, hating myself. By the end of the scene, I was letting her convince me that I didn't want to marry George.

It was the section Annie had trouble with in rehearsals. And I found, like Annie, it felt painful, the way my character was sacrificing herself.

Melanie: *"I'm just not sure what I want anymore."*

Julia: *"You can't get married for them. You have to put yourself first. You have to be selfish."*

Melanie: *"But all the planning . . . the expense . . ."*

Julia: *"You can't think about that!"*

Melanie: *"It would hurt George incredibly!"*

Julia: *"Wouldn't it be worse marrying him when that's not what you really want? Wouldn't that be hurting him much more?"*

Melanie: *"I just . . . I don't know. I don't want to hurt anyone."*

I paused and looked at Julia.

Melanie: *"Why does it feel like whatever I do, someone is going to get hurt?"*

Julia: *"If you want, I'll tell Mom and Dad. And Dad will tell George, and then Mom will call everyone, and it will be just like it was never going to happen."*

Melanie: *"But it's crazy."*

Julia: *"It's okay. If you need to be crazy . . . then be crazy."*

I took a good long moment before answering.

Melanie: *"Okay."*

Julia: *"Are you sure? Because this has to be your decision."*

Melanie: *"Yes."*

Julia: *"Fine. I'll go tell Mom and Dad."*

Kelly walked to the door stage left and paused before exiting.

Julia: *"I'm glad that I'm here to help. After all. That's what sisters are for. Right?"*

She exited, and the lights went out, and I got offstage, relieved to get that scene over with. I wanted to shake myself free of it like a dog jiggles dry after getting wet. But Kelly was changing outfits again, and before I knew it we were back out there in the third scene. It's a year later, and Julia is desperate. It was the same passage Annie had complained about in rehearsal. The one that had been so hard to rewrite. And I realized that I had to go through the feelings again, not just in a coffee shop with a muffin to get me through the words on the page, but out loud in front of an audience.

Julia: *"I've lost my lease. I'll end up on the street. But you don't give a fuck, do you, all you care about is yourself!"*

Melanie: *"How can you say that? Who lent you money when you quit your job and couldn't go a day without getting high? Who stayed up with you night after night because you thought spiders on your shower curtain were going to eat you alive?! I hate you for making me feel this way, Julia! Hate you! And I'm not letting you do it anymore! Because you've never been happy no matter what I do. There was always something making you angry, some injustice, some reason to yell and scream and throw a fit and make everyone around you feel unhappy like we were all doing something wrong."* (I looked up from the script. I knew the rest of the speech by heart.) *"But it wasn't us—it was you. Selfish, egotistical, mentally unbalanced chemically screwed-up you! Well I've spent my life tiptoeing my own needs around you and it never does any good, so just stop asking me for help and leave me alone!"*

Kelly glared at me, fiercely.

Julia: *"Fine. Enjoy having your apartment all to yourself. And don't worry, I'll never ask you for anything, ever again."*

Melanie: *"That sounds good to me!"*

Julia: *"Have a nice life, Melanie."* Kelly paused at the door-way. Turned around. *"I dare you to have a nice life."*

She exited.

Blackout.

Intermission.

As I got offstage I could hear applause from the audience, and when we were safely in the wings, the lights went up. The applause frittered away, and I wondered what everyone out there thought, but I couldn't dwell on it. Kelly and I went backstage without speaking and as soon as I could, I collapsed onto a chair.

Under normal circumstances I like hanging out with ac-tresses at intermission. It's fun to see them switch from their onstage personas to their real selves and then back to their on-stage personas. But there was no way I was going to do that with her now.

Kelly didn't say anything. She drank some water and fixed her makeup. I drank some water too—actually felt the need to "replenish my fluids"—and watched as she put some cream on her face that gave it a kind of white cast.

That's when it dawned on me. The hardest part was still ahead. The so-called infamous "ghost scene." I wondered how Kelly felt now about doing it. Resentful? Or had Peter made it well worth her while?

I looked at myself in the mirror. Thought of putting make-up on, but it was just as well I looked like a wreck. The char-acter was a wreck. Why pretend otherwise? Maybe Kelly had been right. Maybe this scene would be a fiasco. A joke. Idiotic and stupid. I would make a total fool out of myself out there both as writer and actor in one swoop.

Worse yet, maybe the scene would get to me so much I'd break down into uncontrollable sobs in front of everyone.

By now, Kelly had changed into skintight black pants, a

skintight black tank top, and black stilettos. Sure, she was playing someone dead, but she looked great. Powerful.

I put on some lipstick. Carol poked her head in and asked if everything was okay.

"My pits are totally sweaty. Do you know if there's anything I could change into?"

"Here."

She took off the black sweatshirt she was wearing.

"Thanks."

"We'll be starting back up in ten minutes."

I took off my top and put on the sweatshirt. It was just as well that it looked oversized and plain. In this scene I'd be unpacking boxes of Julia's things that I've moved out of her apartment.

Carol poked her head back in. "Places."

My stomach muscles clenched up. While I wanted to contract myself into a little ball, Kelly stood up and stretched out. Took another sip of water. Totally calm. I had to hand it to her. She hadn't gone up on her lines once. As a matter of fact, she'd been doing an incredibly good job. So much for all our angst at dress rehearsal. But it remained to be seen how she would handle this scene.

She didn't look at me or say anything as we went out onstage. I followed. Gripped the script, my life raft, to my chest. I knew that no matter how insecure I felt, in order for this scene to work, just like I'd been willing Annie all along, I had to be a worthy opponent.

We passed by Peter, who was standing by the curtain. I couldn't resist looking at him. Searching out some sort of praise. I was doing like he wanted and I was doing okay, right? Maybe trying a little too hard to act. But it was hard to resist. A little reassurance would've been nice. Just a little smile. That was all I wanted.

But he wasn't looking at me. He was looking at Kelly. And just before she went out onstage, she paused in front of him, and he leaned over, and they kissed each other full on the lips.

And he knew I was looking. He knew!

His eyes followed her out onstage and he never even acknowledged me at all.

I hated him. I hated her. I wanted to kill them both.

The lights came up.

There was the audience. Waiting. Expecting. Nothing to do but begin. We flew through the first pages of the scene, where it gradually becomes apparent that Julia's dead.

Melanie: *"I'm sorry about the things I said. I didn't mean to get so angry."*

Julia: *"But you did get angry, didn't you."*

Melanie: *"I called the next day."*

Julia: *"Not this again."*

Melanie: *"And I left a message."*

Julia: *"We know, we know . . ."*

Melanie: *"And I told you I changed my mind and you could move in."*

Julia: *"But you were too late."*

We continued on through the scene. I was vaguely aware that no one in the audience moved or made a sound.

Melanie: *"There's still the hope that you've just gone on a walk, and you'll be coming up the stairs to your apartment any second, and I'll say, 'God! Julia! Where have you been? I was starting to think. . . !' "*

Julia: *"And I would say, 'Melanie, I'm so happy you've come. If I'd known, I would've made some dinner. Your favorite pasta, with sweet Italian sausage.' "*

Melanie: *"You enjoy this part, don't you."*

Julia: *"You had a standing invitation."*

Melanie: *"The bathroom door was open."*

Julia: *"But I wasn't standing."*

I paused. I wasn't sure if I could get through this speech. Felt my chest tighten. Tried to breathe. To force my voice out. It was barely above a whisper. Dead quiet in the theater. Except for my voice.

Melanie: *"You were sitting on the floor, leaning against the tile wall. Limp. Like a marionette without its strings. In your white slip. The pink bath mat pushed up against the tub. Like you'd slipped. Slipped in your slip. Your eyes open and your face white . . . and you had this . . . frown."*

I looked at Kelly. Her face was hard. She'd never liked this speech because she never knew what she was supposed to be doing while Melanie was saying it.

My eyes searched her out, and she looked away. Yes, I thought. Look away. *"Like you were very angry. No, not angry. Just very . . . sad. And I backed out of the room. And sunk down onto your unmade bed. And said your name out loud. 'Julia.' I wanted to talk to you. 'Look what's happened! Look what you did!' But we would never be able to talk about it. I would never be able to tell you . . . you're dead."*

And then Kelly started to circle me, singing that song from *White Christmas.* *" 'Sister, sisters, there were never such devoted sisters, Never had to have a chaperone, no sir. I'm there to keep my eye on her. . . .' "*

Melanie: *"It's my fault, isn't it. I wouldn't let you move in with me. I said such horrible things. And you went home angry, hating me . . ."*

Julia: (still singing) *" 'Sharing, caring, ev'ry little thing that we are wearing. When a certain gentleman arrived from Rome, she wore the dress and—' "*

Melanie: *"You got some pills out of the medicine cabinet. And you took them; you took them all! And you thought, 'This will show her!'"*

Julia: *"Have a nice life, Melanie."*

Melanie: *"Tell me you didn't do it!"*

Julia: *"I dare you to have a nice life."*

I stood up. A change in Melanie's strength here. Now I started to circle her.

Melanie: *"I wish . . ."*

Julia: *"Be careful . . ."*

Melanie: *"I wish . . ."*

Julia: *"Be careful!"*

Melanie: *"I wish you had never been born."*

Julia: *"Uh huh."*

Melanie: *"And your misery never had the chance to be felt!"*

Julia: *"I can't believe it! The little coward is finally going to tell us how she feels!"*

I looked at Kelly. Kelly, not Julia.

Because that was not the line I wrote. And as I seriously considered saying, *What the fuck are you doing?* she grabbed my script and threw it on the bed and smirked at me.

Maybe there was something honorable somewhere in her intentions. Maybe she wanted to get my head out of the script so I would stop using it as a crutch. But I wasn't puzzling out her motives right then. I wanted to kill her. And I was regretting not having a weapon. But the audience was waiting. And it happened that I knew my line. I wasn't sure if I knew the whole speech, and it was a big one, but I thought I might, and I felt compelled to deliver it instead of killing her, so I took the plunge.

Melanie: *"I have lived . . . my entire life . . . with your unhappiness looming over me. Like a stunted little scraggly bush growing under the shade of a gigantic overgrown tree with huge fat branches that snake around me like tentacles sucking the life out of me. I wanted your suffering out of my way, out of my life. I wanted you dead! Dead and gone! Because if you had never lived. Just imagine. My life. It would've been an entirely different story!"*

I stood there frozen, feeling like lightning would strike me dead.

Julia: *"Ladies and gentlemen. Our prime suspect has finally confessed."*

Melanie: *"I wished you dead and you died."*

Julia: *"So you get the credit?"*

Melanie: *"Guilty as charged. Case closed."*

Julia: *"As if your guilt could solve anything."*

Melanie: *"I'm sorry."*

Julia: *"Your guilt is useless."*

Melanie: *"I am responsible for your death!"*

Kelly laughed and walked to the door.

Melanie: *"Where are you going?"*

Julia: *"Out of your mind."*

Melanie: *"You can't go, Julia."*

Julia: *"I'm sorry."*

Melanie: *"I won't let you!"*

Julia: *"You don't have any choice."*

Melanie: *"Please don't go!"*

And she opened the door. And she exited. And she closed the door behind her. And the set didn't fall over. And I sat down on the bed. And the lights went down. And everything was black for a moment. And then everything was bright again. And Kelly was standing next to me and we faced the audience and everyone was applauding.

And it was over.

Thank God.

What a relief.

Immediately, my whole body started to shake again and I thought my knees were going to give out as I took a bow.

It was bizarre to be standing up there in front of the applause instead of hiding in the last row behind it. All those faces smiling at me. I smiled back.

Clapping is such a ridiculous gesture, I always think. People acting like a bunch of stupid trained seals. But how sweet a sound it is when they're applauding for you. And then Kelly turned and clapped for me too. Smiling. We hugged. Look what we did together!

I have to say. Nothing in my life had ever been so thrilling as when I delivered the last two pages of dialogue without my script. My sister, I thought, she would've been proud.

Well, maybe not proud. Annoyed, more likely, to have to share the spotlight.

But a little proud.

Carol brought us each a bouquet of flowers. Pink roses. Peter must've gotten them. I felt a little guilty, as I breathed in the sweet scent, that I hadn't brought any for the others. Oh well. I got my own.

And finally we left the stage, and Carol was nudging me— "I bet you're gonna want to be an actress now, huh!"

"No way, no way!"

And Rocco Shorenstein, a rotund man in his 60s (of course) was already backstage with Peter. Peter looking very nervous. "Where is she?" Rocco was saying, "Very moving. A very moving play. I want to meet this talented young woman!"

I almost had a coronary. Was someone in a position to do something amazing with my career actually telling me that I was talented?

"This is the playwright, of course," Peter said, indicating me, "and—"

"There she is!" Rocco said, going straight to Kelly. He shook her hand so vehemently she almost dropped her flowers. "You are going to be famous one day, my dear!" he proclaimed.

And she laughed and said oh so politely, "Why thank you."

"You were fantastic!"

"Thank you so much."

"And this," said Peter, "is the playwright, Jennifer Ward."

"Very moving play. You did a good job out there, sweetie. And the writing is excellent." (He didn't shake my hand.) "So what," Rocco said, turning to Peter, "do you all plan to do with it? What's the next step?"

"Well, we have a month to run," Peter said, "and we hope to get some reviews, and of course we hope to find a producer who would be interested in moving it to a larger theater."

"I wish you all the luck in the world," Rocco said. "It's a fine play. They certainly should do more plays like that on Broadway. But, you know, they don't like dramas. Unless it's Miller, or maybe Mamet, but other than that it's musicals and comedies, and even those are tough, unless you're Neil Simon, and even he's having a rough time filling houses these days."

"We'd settle for Off Broadway," I said, surprised to hear my own voice enter the conversation, but I was feeling heady from the performance, "but it never hurts to be ambitious."

"Never hurts to be ambitious, right you are little lady!" he said. "That last scene," he turned to Kelly, "when you came back as a ghost! Fantastic! So theatrical! I love it!"

He was saying this to her as if she had thought it up. And there she was, smiling, taking credit. I fought off the urge to tell Rocco how she'd thrown a fit to have it changed, walked out on rehearsals, slept with Peter . . .

"Just riveting!" he raved on. "Do you have an agent?"

"Bernie Warner," she said, "at ICM."

"Then I want you to have Bernie give me a call tomorrow morning. I've got a part for you in my next play."

"Thank you. I'll have him call. Thank you so much."

"Nice job, all of you." He deigned to look at me. "It's tough out there, but don't give up. Keep on writing. You never know what's going to happen."

"Thank you for coming, Mr. Shorenstein," Peter said, "I'll walk you out."

And Rocco gave one last look to Kelly. "Call me."

"I will."

And he left, escorted by Peter.

"So," Kelly said. "How does the playwright feel?"

"That was the most horrible experience of my life," I said.

"And you loved every minute of it," she said back.

And I had to agree.

The cast and crew went to Rosie O'Grady's and sat at a big round table in the back. As I looked over the menu that I knew so well, I started to come back down to earth, and became aware of feeling a bit odd to be celebrating. It seemed like it was to some extent at my sister's expense. But I knew there would be more than enough time to inflict guilt on myself later, so I pushed the thought to the back of my mind and ordered a huge plate of chicken fingers and a bottle of light beer.

Just as we were all toasting the play, Annie came running in. "I knew I'd find you all here. What happened?! Did you do it? Who went on in my place?!"

"We put in a call to Drew Barrymore and she happened to be available," Carol said.

"I hope she's not going to replace me."

"She wanted to, but we said no," Peter said, standing up to pull a chair in for her. "Because the playwright herself decided to step in."

"You!" she screamed, looking at me. "I don't believe it."

"Neither do I."

"So are you going to be an actress now?"

Kelly burst out laughing. "You should've seen how nervous she was! Her body was having its own private earthquake."

"I am so glad that's over with," I said to Annie. "Don't you dare miss another performance."

But thank you, I thought, for missing just this one.

*   *   *

I didn't know if Kelly left with Peter. I didn't want to know. I left before they did and went home to collapse in my bed.

The next day, I was looking forward to getting to watch a full performance of the play and not actually have to be in it. I still hadn't gotten to see the whole thing through without stopping.

I suppose I was still hoping that whatever had gone on between Peter and Kelly was an aberration. That he would wake up the next day horrified by what he'd done, tell her their night of sex had been a big mistake, and plead for my forgiveness.

But when I got there early, no one was in the lobby, and Peter wasn't in his office, and I heard voices in the theater. So I went in, and Peter and Kelly were sitting there together in the front row. He had his arm draped over her shoulder. She was laughing.

I turned myself around and went back to the elevator and let myself out onto the street. At least I hadn't made a sound. No one had seen me. No one knew I'd been there. And my presence wasn't expected, so I wouldn't be missed. At this point, as a matter of fact, there was no reason for me to show my face again. I'd gone from being the absolute center of attention the night before—to being irrelevant.

It was depressing. But it was satisfying too. My play existed without me—it had taken on a life of its own.

But I was fooling myself if I thought I'd be able to stay away. Curiosity drove me back the very next night. I timed it out to get there just after they began. I didn't want to have to relate to anyone. I just wanted to watch.

Beth was there closing down the box office. "Hey," she said, "where have you been?"

"Around."

"Well guess what. You're sold out."

"Really?"

"Not a seat in the house. You should've seen the line I had going out the door!"

"Wow. That's great," I said, though I could hear my voice sound stilted.

"You look disappointed."

"I'm not. Really. It's just, I was going to watch the show tonight."

"Oh. Well, you could stand in the back I guess."

"I guess."

As Beth put the money in an envelope, I listened to Kelly's voice waft in from the theater. *"Not to mention, it keeps the wolves at bay. On the fifth floor there's always the danger of someone breaking in from the roof."*

"Maybe I'll just sit out here and listen," I said, sinking into the sofa.

"Suit yourself," Beth said, taking the money into Peter's office and then reappearing a minute later. "Good night."

"Good night. Thanks."

"Enjoy the show."

They got through the first act beautifully. I didn't even miss not seeing it. The play seemed like a poem to me that night. The dialogue flowed seamlessly and rhythmically, with no extra air, no extra words. It was the first time I'd heard it through as it was meant to be heard. It didn't really matter that I couldn't see them. I could picture them just fine in my head.

As people applauded for intermission, I headed out the door. I still didn't want to make any contact with people, so I took a walk and bought some M & Ms and then returned to the lobby just as the last few people straggled back into the theater. I was enjoying this feeling of sneaking in to see my own play with no one knowing I was there. But then, towards the end of the second act, Peter emerged from his office.

"Hello," he said. "I didn't know you were out here."

"Hello," I said. "I didn't know you were in there."

We kept our voices low so the audience wouldn't hear.

"You've got a sold out show tonight," he said. "And about half of them are actually paying customers."

"I heard. It must be nice for the actresses to have a full house to perform to."

"Oh, yeah. I bet they're loving it."

I returned to my listening, and didn't really look at him, but from the corner of my eye I saw him hesitate before sitting down next to me. It became hard to concentrate on the play with him sitting so close.

I imagined a conversation with him in my mind. In my mind, I asked him how he could break off our flirtation and succumb to Kelly's lower animal nature. And he told me he hated himself for it. He told me his attraction to her made him feel weak and dirty, and I was the one he really wanted to feel weak and dirty with.

And then Peter said, "There's something I've been wanting to ask you."

"Yes?"

"Are you pleased with the production?"

"Yes."

"I hope you don't regret allowing me to direct your play."

"Of course not. You've done a wonderful job."

"Thanks. I'm glad you feel that way."

Neither of us spoke for a moment. The play was coming to its climax.

Melanie: *"I wish . . ."*

Julia: *"Be careful . . ."*

Melanie: *"I wish . . ."*

Julia: *"Be careful!"*

Melanie: *"I wish you had never been born."*

Julia: *"Uh huh."*

Melanie: *"And your misery never had the chance to be felt!"*

"Can I ask you something?" I said.

"Sure."

"Why did you do it?"

"Your play?"

"Kelly."

He paused before he answered. "She's a very seductive woman."

"I thought you felt something for me."

"I do."

"But that doesn't mean anything?"

"I don't know. Does it?"

I felt confused. It seemed like *he* was accusing *me*. Did it all boil down to the fact that I didn't sleep with him that night? And he was a healthy red-blooded boy and what could I expect?

"I know I'm not perfect," I said.

"I don't expect you to be."

"I don't understand."

"What?"

The actresses were nearing the end of the play.

Julia: *"Ladies and gentlemen. Our prime suspect has finally confessed."*

"You don't even seem to be guilty," I said.

"Why should I be guilty?"

"I'm not saying you necessarily should be. I just thought maybe you would be."

Melanie: *"I wished you dead and you died."*

"This guilt thing," Peter said, "people like us need to stop inflicting it on ourselves, don't you think?"

Julia: *"As if your guilt could solve anything."*

"Yes," I agreed. "It's important to have a good time while we're here."

"If you can," Peter said.

Melanie: *"I am responsible for your death!"*

It crossed my mind to say that if it was just about the sex, we could get together that night with a copy of the Kama Sutra and try every position in the book. But I wasn't sure I could back that up. In any case, I felt sufficiently bewildered by his attitude that I didn't know what else to say.

"I'm sorry things worked out like this," I said. "With us, I mean. Not the play."

"Me too," he said.

I was trying to puzzle out why we weren't together if we were both sorry things hadn't worked out. And I was going to ask him that very question. But my ears wanted to hear Melanie's final desperate plea.

Melanie: *"You can't go, Julia."*

Julia: *"I'm sorry."*

Melanie: *"I won't let you!"*

Julia: *"You don't have any choice."*

Melanie: *"Please don't go!"*

I could see, in my mind's eye, Kelly leaving the stage. And Melanie sitting on the bed. And the lights coming down.

The audience started to clap and Peter excused himself to open the door so they could funnel out. As I headed down the stairs, they were still getting a nice round of applause.

We did get one review. Someone from the *Village Voice* came during the third week of the run. I was sure she would write something about the evil younger sister's evil thoughts. But she didn't. She said I truly captured the way two sisters relate to each other. And she praised the direction. And she called the two actresses' performances a "tour de force." I was especially glad for Annie since this was her first review. But it appeared too late in the run to do us any practical good.

By the last weekend of the run, I decided I could let my parents come. My mother cried a lot and gave me a hug afterwards. My father said it was very touching. I didn't want them to give me any sort of critical evaluation, and I was glad they didn't try. I wondered if the play made them perceive me differently. But I didn't ask. I didn't want to violate the pretense that it was all made up and had nothing to do whatsoever with my own personal experiences.

Even though I did a big mailing to agents, none ever showed up. Not even the guy who had once sort of been my agent, even though I left him three messages, so I figured he was now my official ex-agent.

Two or three more producers did come. From the feedback Peter got, I understood they thought the play was pretty good. As good if not better than many of the dramas currently running Off Broadway. But no one wanted to move it. The subject matter was "too depressing." "Hard to sell." "Would need a big name to get it going."

"So how do we get a big name?" I asked Peter, the last night of the show. We were all at Rosie O'Grady's. I felt like I needed to make one last attempt to keep my play alive. And to keep my play for Peter alive.

"It's rough. If you want a name, and you send it to their agent, the agent will probably send it back unread."

"Even if it's a good vehicle?"

"The last thing an agent wants is for their client to get involved with a theater project. There's no money in it!"

"But isn't there some prestige involved and that can be good for their career?"

"Yes, but you could only begin to get their attention by telling them we have a big producer involved. Not Peter Heller with his fifty-seat house."

"So why doesn't one of these big producers take the play to a big name since they're the ones who have the power to do that?"

"You know, Jennifer . . ." he said, with a mixture of amusement and annoyance, "we tried our goddamned best. But you can't force anyone to produce a play."

And that seemed to be the end of it.

For me. And for my play.

But not for Kelly.

Because Rocco did put her in his next production on Broadway. And she got her *New York Times* rave review. Which led to her getting the part on the sitcom *Baby Makes Three* and then landing the part in *I Told You So* with Brad Pitt. Which led to her part in *Body Beautiful*. Which led to her surprising everyone (as a total newcomer to the Hollywood scene) by being nominated for an Academy Award—up against Winona Ryder, Cameron Diaz, Julianne Moore and Catherine Zeta-Jones.

After the show closed, we all said we would stay in touch. And we all went our separate ways. So I didn't know what happened with Kelly and Peter. And I didn't want to know. Actually, I was dying to know. But I wasn't going to do anything to find out.

Chapter
13

About two years after my play closed, I tuned in when Kelly was being interviewed by Jay Leno. She was publicizing her movie *Body Beautiful*. And she mentioned how much she missed acting in the theater, and how that was really her first love, blah blah blah. They always say that. Of course she didn't mention me or my play. Not that I expected she would. But it would've been fun if she had.

Not that my entire life came to a complete standstill because Kelly became a movie star and I remained a regular person. Okay, maybe I felt on some level like it did. But I continued to exist. I continued to write. I continued to send out my plays. And I did have a few small productions here and there. Not at any place anyone would've heard of. But enough to keep me from giving up.

I didn't give up on becoming a full-fledged sexual person, either. I went out with a few guys. But as far as the sex was concerned, it wasn't very good and there wasn't much of it. Part of my problem was, I couldn't find anyone who really interested me as much as Peter and Kelly.

It was soon after I saw *Body Beautiful* that I decided I had to do something about myself. So I bought a few books on female sexuality. (Thank god for anonymous online ordering.) And I attempted, once again, the challenge of masturbating.

One of the books talked a lot about the importance of having a positive voice inside your head. So I turned my lights down, got into bed naked, and prepared myself for Diana. I knew she'd be there waiting to taunt me. And I was right. But this time, when she started in, I replaced her with Kelly's voice. And Kelly was much more encouraging. "Don't feel guilty," she told me. "There's nothing wrong with enjoying yourself. Everyone else is. Why shouldn't you? Nothing bad is going to happen. Go ahead. Do it."

And I did.

I was surprised how easy it was to quiet Diana. It made me think about how I was getting used to her absence. My memory of her was becoming more vague. Which was a relief. But it was distressing, too. I didn't want to lose her completely. So I took out a copy of *Til Death Do Us Part* and started to read. It was the first time I'd looked at that play since the production. I was sure it would bring Diana back to me. But it was Kelly I saw saying the lines, Kelly's voice I heard. Diana was receding into the past, and there was nothing I could do about it.

It was about three years after my production of *Til Death Do Us Part* that Kelly was back in New York doing *Betrayal* on Broadway. I had a play of my own going up on 42nd Street way over near Eleventh Avenue in a small theater called the Matrix.

It had been a pleasant surprise when Jack, the resident director at the theater, called me about a script I'd sent in for a contest they were holding (no money prize, only glory) and told me he loved my play and wanted to produce it.

We met for coffee at the Kraft, a Greek coffee shop on

Tenth Avenue. If I had any fantasies about falling in love with my director again, it wouldn't be this time. Jack was a very sweet man in his late 50s who stuttered and dressed a bit like a homeless person. He did once direct Julie Andrews on Broadway and some episodes of *Gilligan's Island*. (No job security in this business, that's for sure.)

We had a nice conversation about our mutual addiction to the soap opera *All My Children*. His live-in girlfriend had a small recurring part on the show as a nanny. Then he launched into a speech about how much he loved my play. His enthusiasm seduced me, and I couldn't say no.

My play *Copy Cat* was a three-character romantic comedy about two women and a guy who work in an advertising agency. It was a love triangle and completely invented.

Okay. Actually, it was loosely based on a romantic triangle I had the chance to observe in the law office where I worked because all our desks were in one big room and everyone knew everyone else's business.

Okay. I was one of the people involved in the love triangle.

Okay. It didn't have anything to do with anyone at my job at the law office. It was all about Peter and Kelly and me.

The ninty-nine-seat Matrix Theater had been around forever, and it smelled like it. Years of leaking pipes, mildew, cigarette smoke, lack of ventilation, and dust accumulation made it a bit hard to breathe. And they could've budgeted some money towards buying duct tape to repair the torn vinyl seats. But it was a few blocks from my apartment, so at least it was easy to get there.

Rehearsals were going well. We'd survived the lead actor quitting (I didn't know why he did and never would). And we were still looking for someone to do props (for no pay). And we were having some arguments over the set (Salvation Army shoddy). But unless I was willing to shell out to pay for office furniture myself, I was stuck with it. Otherwise, I was looking forward to opening night a few days away. I walked home, happy to stretch my legs and get some real air to breathe after sitting in the stuffy theater all afternoon.

In Manhattan, it's fairly common to run into old acquaintances on the street. Sooner or later you're just bound to cross paths with everyone you once knew. Especially if it's someone you've had a fight with. Or someone you've avoided because the relationship came to an unpleasant resolution. Or unpleasant lack of resolution. Sometimes you walk by this person and pretend you don't see them. And you wonder if they saw you too, and if they're pretending not to see you too, and what they think about the fact that maybe you saw them and are pretending not to see them too. But when Peter and I saw each other on the corner of Ninth Avenue and 42th Street we did not pretend not to see each other.

"Hello!"

"Hi!"

"How have you been!"

"Good! How have you been?"

"Fine!"

"Great."

We were surrounded by zillions of cars and people, but we forged ahead with one of those stupid conversations where you're being friendly, but not friendly enough that you would actually say "Let's go have a cup of coffee" and find out anything of any depth and it's like you're both going to say goodbye any second, but then you keep saying more things about yourself, some of them potentially important even, but it's all in a rushed, throw-away tone.

"Still writing plays?"

"Yes, of course. How's the directing going?"

"Great. I was living up in Connecticut for a year. Did a couple seasons at Hartford Rep."

"Annie told me. I saw her once at Barnes and Noble."

"Oh, yeah. I saw her at a Starbucks downtown. Man, you leave for a year, come back, and these Starbucks have sprouted every few blocks."

"Yeah. It's crazy." *And Oh God*, we're both thinking, *why do we have to have this stupid conversation—we should've just pretended not to see each other and walked on.* "So," I asked, raising my voice above the sound of a huge mack truck, "are you involved in a production right now?"

"I have one coming up," he said, nodding like he knew that question was next. "At the Blue Light."

"That's a good theater. They have a lot of LA movie star connections there, don't they?"

"It keeps them well financed, yeah. It's nice not to be the producer on a show, and you can just concentrate on the directing."

"I bet. You should send me a flier."

"I will. Still at the same address?"

"Yep."

"I don't suppose you've done any more acting," he teased me.

"Oh, God, no."

He looked towards the intersection and I thought he was going to say that he had to catch the light. But then he said, "So do you have any productions in the works?"

I hesitated slightly. I wanted to resist telling him. Because if he got the bright idea of coming to *Copy Cat* (not that he would bother, but what if he did?) it would be incredibly embarrassing for him to see that I had written about him.

"Oh, well, a small one. It's opening next week."

Stupid vanity! I had to tell him, just so he wouldn't think I had nothing going on.

"Great. I'll try to come see it."

"No! You shouldn't bother. The production is really not good."

"I'm sure you're just being modest. Why don't you send me a flier?" he asked.

"Really, we've been having lots of problems . . ."

"I know all about those kind of problems. Don't worry about it—you know I love your work. What's it about?"

"Oh, you know, the play—it just isn't worth coming to, Peter, really. When I have something good, I'll invite you, I promise, but this . . . It's a horrible production. Don't waste your time."

"Okay. Well. Good luck with it. And let me know when you have something going up that you'd like me to see."

"I will. And good luck to you too." And then, I wasn't going to ask, but it just came out. "By the way. Do you ever still speak to Kelly?"

Just then a scruffy looking teenage boy came up to us asking for spare change but we both shook our heads and thank god he walked on.

"I did see Kelly a couple times over the years, but it's hard to stay in touch."

"Yeah."

"You know how it goes. After her career took off . . ."

"Right," I said, wondering if she'd dumped him unceremoniously and how much he'd suffered.

"I'm thinking of seeing her in *Betrayal*," he said.

"So am I. But tickets are so expensive."

"It's crazy, isn't it?"

He put his hand on my elbow, and I thought he wanted to touch me, for touching sake, and maybe he was about to say something along the lines of . . . *I never really wanted her, it was you all along, Jennifer* . . . but then I realized he was trying to move me over because a woman with a baby stroller was trying to get by.

"Pretty amazing what's happening with her," I said, stepping aside.

"Yes. Pretty amazing. And we knew her when."

"We knew her when . . ."

"Well. Anyway. It's good to see you."

"It's good to see you too. Send me your flier."

"I will. Take care, Jennifer."

"Take care."

I felt like I did see something sad behind his eyes. Like he did want to say more. But he didn't say more. And I didn't say more. And we both went our separate ways.

And that's when I found myself heading to the Helen Hayes Theater a few blocks away to see about buying tickets to *Betrayal* starring Kelly Cavanna.

I wasn't going to buy a ticket. I just wanted to scope it out. See what they were charging. See the posters of her out front.

When I reached the theater, there was a life-size picture of Kelly behind the glass. She was in a white dress and smiling just like a movie star. There was no line to buy tickets, so I walked up to the guy in the little cagelike box office in the lobby and asked him what kind of seats were available in the next few weeks. Not because I was going to buy one, but just because I felt bad for him sitting there with nothing to do, and I was curious to see how well ticket sales were going. An orchestra seat cost seventy-five dollars, which seemed outrageous. No play was worth that. He told me he could probably find me a single in the orchestra any night I wanted to go. So I asked him to check for Tuesday of the following week (just to see) and he told me that for that performance, he had an excellent seat in the third row near the center. Wow, I thought. Close enough to catch her spit. So I took it.

Copy Cat had three characters. The fake me. The fake Peter. And the fake Kelly. The audience was full. We were doing our first "preview," which meant we hadn't officially opened yet. The people in the seats were mostly "papered," meaning the tickets were given away free to organizations like The Village Nursing Home, the Gay Men's Health Clinic, NYU Student Services . . . The hope was that they might start to spread a little positive word of mouth so that actual paying people might eventually come.

I was feeling too tense to watch the play. The really scary thing about a comedy is wondering if anyone is going to laugh. Because if the play fails—it fails loudly. With silence. The loudest silence in the world. And it's the worst feeling, to sit through your play, which was meant to get people to laugh, and see them frowning like they're sitting through *Death of a Salesman*. So if no one was going to laugh, I didn't want to be stuck in the theater suffering, so even though there were empty seats inside, I stayed in the lobby and listened.

When the laughter came, it seemed like a miracle. They got my weird sense of humor! They didn't hate the grungy office furniture! They weren't puking from the foul smelling air!

I didn't go in to watch the play until the last five minutes. I couldn't resist seeing the end. I stood in the back, in the aisle, and smiled.

Gabrielle: *"It seems like the art director shouldn't get involved with his copywriter."*

Paul: *"You think so?"*

Gabrielle: *"Yeah, because then they'll just want you to hire them to write the copy for all their ads."*

Paul: *"Are you being sarcastic?"*

Gabrielle: *"What do you mean?"*

Paul: *"Because we are involved."*

Gabrielle: *"We are?"*

Paul: *"Aren't we?"*

Gabrielle: *"Well . . . I'm not sure if we are or not. Aren't you madly in love with Kiki?"*

Paul: *"Why would you think that?"*

Gabrielle: *"Why wouldn't I think that? I mean, she's beautiful and sexy and I'm just a boring, sexually repressed copywriter . . ."*

Paul: *"Maybe YOU should sleep with her."*

Gabrielle: *"So . . . you aren't madly in love with her?"*

Paul: *"Beautiful blondes like her, they're always so full of themselves. It gets on my nerves."*

Gabrielle: *"Really."*

Paul: *"So anyway, I'd better go."*

Gabrielle: *"So soon?"*

Paul: *"I'm exhausted. And tomorrow is a big day. We do have that presentation first thing in the morning and I really need to get some rest."*

Gabrielle: *"Why don't you get some rest . . . here?"*

Paul: *"Here?"*

Gabrielle: *"I live so close to the office. It'll save you the subway ride tomorrow morning."*

Paul: *"Is that the only reason you're offering?"*

Gabrielle: *"No. As a matter of fact . . ."*

Paul: *"Yes?"*

Gabrielle: *"The truth is . . ."*

Paul: *"Yes?"*

Gabrielle: *"I'm in love with you, Paul. I've been in love with you since the day we met. And you interviewed me. And I thought you weren't going to give me the job, but then you did . . ."*

Paul: *"You're kidding!"*

Gabrielle: *"No!"*

Paul: *"But I've been in love with you ever since the day I interviewed you and I wasn't going to give you the job but then I did . . ."*

Gabrielle: *"So does that mean you'll get involved with me? Even though I write the copy for your ads?"*

Paul: *"Like I said . . . I'm already involved with you."* (pause) *"Just don't expect me to approve all your copy."*

Gabrielle: *"Oh, no. I would never do that."*

(They kiss. Blackout.)

And there was applause. And I clapped too. It felt so satisfying, how they ended up together.

Unfortunately, as the actors came out to take their curtain call, the lights were still down. Jack motioned for Cal, the guy up in the lighting booth, to turn them up. But they didn't come up. And the actors took another bow in the dark, and then left the stage shaking their heads and swearing.

The houselights came up, and people left the theater. It was hard to tell what they had thought of the play, since they were all talking about the fact that the actors had taken a curtain call in the dark.

Cal didn't usually make mistakes like that, so I followed Jack up the steep steps to the lighting booth to see what happened. And there, to my surprise, sitting with Cal . . . was Peter.

I must've looked as horrified as I was.

"Hi, Jennifer!" He was grinning.

"Peter—" I started to say, but Jack interrupted me.

"What the hell happened?!"

"Sorry about that little problem at the end," Cal said.

I imagined they were so busy laughing—not at the play, but at me and what I'd written—that he'd forgotten his cue.

"The light blew. I'll change it as soon as the theater empties out," he said.

"Cal is an old friend of mine," Peter said. "He mentioned he was doing lights for your play. I hope you don't mind . . ."

"So you saw it?"

"Sure. I watched from up here. It was great," he said. "Very funny. Cal and I were laughing the whole way through."

(Laughing at me . . .)

"Oh, good, well . . ." But I didn't know what to say. I'd already said too much—in the play. And now I was truly tongue tied.

He looked into my eyes then, and my fantasies went on overdrive. Maybe he saw now that I had always wanted to profess my love to him, and now that Gabrielle had done it onstage in front of everyone, he saw that I'd just been too shy to get it out, and maybe he had always wanted to say that to me too, and now maybe he would ask me out for a bite to eat, and we'd admit our love for each other and go back to one of our apartments and do our very own seduction scene that very night!

"Congratulations," he said, "on your play. Good to see you again."

"You too."

Chapter
14

As soon as I stepped into the Helen Hayes Theater and found my way to my red velvet third row orchestra seat, I was so happy that I had come. Not just because of the excitement of seeing Kelly. (Even if I did hate her—proximity to fame inspires forgiveness.) I do love going to a Broadway play if I can manage to forget the rip-off ($75!) price of the ticket. So I settled into my seat and took in my surroundings with pleasure and tried not to compare the whole sumptuous atmosphere of this chandeliered, high-ceilinged, gold-trimmed cherub-decorated theater to the crummy little smelly dump where my own play ($12.50) was being done.

I love going alone. Going alone to the theater is very intimate. It's like the play is your date.

I paged nervously through my Playbill and looked for Kelly's biography. I hoped against hope that she would mention *Til Death Do Us Part* in her credits, even though I knew she wouldn't. My eyes scanned down the blurb, and of course it wasn't there, no surprise, of course.

So I closed my Playbill and scanned the audience. Just one row of these dressed-up theatergoers would fill the whole audience at the Matrix Theater. But I told myself not to torture myself with envy as I waited for the lights to go down. This should be fun, to sit in the dark and observe her. Nothing required of me but to watch and to listen.

And finally the lights did come down, and the curtain went up, and there was that moment I love when the entire audience falls completely silent in communal anticipation of the story that's about to seduce them in.

And there she was. Sitting at a cafe table with Fred Harris, an actor who'd done a lot of theater in New York but had not yet broken into movies. I wondered how he felt about their *New York Times* review. He'd been almost completely ignored. It had to be annoying. I'd been hoping that Kelly would get panned. After all, she'd left me in the dust—why should she get all the fame and glory? But the review was fawning. Glowing. Disgusting. And now she was center stage, beautiful as ever in a white chiffon dress that came to just below her knees and white high heels.

I love how it adds that extra dimension when you watch someone you know in a play. I don't think you ever fully separate them from the part, just like you can't separate the movie star from the part, as if you know the movie star like you know a friend. And here she was both movie star and friend. Or ex-friend. She did seem slimmer than I remembered. More angular, less voluptuous. Her agent, I thought, must not be letting her eat cake.

The play proceeded in its crisp, clear, clever way, going backwards in time starting from when the lovers break up to the moment they first realize they're going to have an affair. Kelly faked a British accent. Not perfectly, but good enough. I tried not to think about whether I would stay after to say hello to her. But the worry kept intruding into my thoughts, and I found it hard to immerse myself into the play.

When intermission came, I stayed by my seat and listened in on people's conversations around me. Nobody was talking about the play. They were talking about problems at work. The line at the bathroom. Where to go for dinner after the show . . .

I tried not to think about my own worry—to stay or not to stay after the show. What if she didn't remember who I was? What if she remembered, but didn't want to see me. What if I went to see her, and she brushed me off because of a pending dinner date with Russell Crowe or George Clooney or whoever she was having a torrid affair with these days?

Finally the lights flickered and people returned to their seats and the play resumed. I tried to pay attention, but I knew the story too well (saw the movie) and was consumed with my own anxieties. The man in front of me was dozing, chin to chest, not snoring thank god. He didn't wake up until the play was over and the audience broke into noisy applause.

When the actors came out to take their bows, lots of people stood up to applaud. That always makes me smile. It seems less about wanting to show appreciation to the actors than the wish to perform the role of audience member to the hilt. Plus, the audience could feel like what they saw was really, really, really great—a performance that will go down in history. They've gotten their money's worth.

But even if I had felt compelled to stand, I wouldn't have. Because I still wasn't sure if I was going to stay to talk to her. And I didn't want her to spot me. She was less than twenty feet away. Flanked by both the male actors, Kelly smiled and bowed regally to the audience. Hoping I would avoid her gaze, I squinched down in my seat like an escaped prisoner avoids the sweep of a searchlight. Finally the applause started to level off, and the actors got off the stage before it would be gone completely, and the curtain came down, and I was left with my dilemma.

I got up from my red velvet seat and made my way to the exit along with the rest of the audience.

The fresh air and the crowds and the traffic thick with cabs and limos jolted me awake. I paused to get my bearings. The street seemed as much like a stage set as what I'd just left. After all, Manhattan was just an island with trees on it before everyone came and built high-rises, right?

I stood on the sidewalk shivering. Not from the cold, but from nervousness. It was zero hour. Time to decide. Stay or go. It would be so much easier just to walk off into the night. Facing her wasn't worth the anxiety. It was as if I was having stage fright. And we were lacking a script, and I didn't know what we might say.

The other thing that made me nervous—and I don't even want to mention it because it's so ridiculous—was that I had this sense of her being a "celebrity." Even though I knew her when she was "a regular person" and I had all sorts of reasons not to think very highly of her. I couldn't help myself. She had been elevated to something beyond normal personhood, and I felt in awe.

As I was standing there, a line started to form along a police barricade that one of the stagehands had set up outside the stage door. A whole contingent of fans was gathering quite enthusiastically and without conflicted feelings to see Kelly Cavanna the movie star. Most of them gripped a pen and a Playbill open to the page with her photo. I shook my head and smiled. They wanted her autograph. Little did they all know, I thought with pride, she had once been in my play. And I had once been in her bed.

Now I was feeling curious. Just to see Kelly come out and sign autographs was worth the price of admission and would probably be more entertaining than *Betrayal*, no offense to Harold Pinter. So I decided to wait. And watch. That still didn't mean I'd have to say anything to her.

So I stood a few feet back from the rest (the fans, the plebes, the common people) who were crowding the sidewalk and tried to be careful not to step off the curb and get hit by a car passing behind me on the street.

And I waited.

It took fifteen minutes before the two male actors appeared. They graciously signed autographs, though no one was really interested in them and we all knew it. It was Kelly Cavanna they'd come to see.

When she finally did come out about ten minutes later, the crowd broke into applause. She smiled and nodded, and I imagined that her ego must be incredibly bloated, especially considering it had been pretty puffed up in the first place.

She was wearing tight black leather pants and a gold tube top with silvery threads woven through it and gold high-heeled sandals. Her makeup had been removed and she looked tired. But she gracefully stopped to sign autographs and chat with all her admirers in line behind the barrier.

I looked down at my Playbill and then back at her. Even I could see, having come this far, that I really should go say hello. It would be totally idiotic not to. I would always regret it. So I tried to talk myself into it. Just say hello and compliment her performance. That's all. Nothing fancy. I didn't have to chastise her for sleeping with Peter or for leaving me off her bio or not mentioning me on Jay Leno or forgetting that I existed. Just a simple hello and good-bye. That was all.

The honk of a cab racing by—passing less than a foot behind me—gave me the charge I needed. The rude blare of the horn made me jump, and I used that momentum to make my way to Kelly.

I approached the police barrier—not so crowded now. And I stood there feeling like a fool. And I waited for her to make her way down the rest of the line.

It was after she finished a conversation with a woman from

Indiana who wanted the autograph for her twelve-year-old daughter who had a poster of Kelly in her room, and Kelly said how sweet that was and signed the woman's program, that out of the corner of her eye she saw me standing there. I smiled.

She registered surprise and then said "Jennifer!"

And I felt like a real big shot in front of everyone else because SHE KNEW ME. And not only that, she came to me and KISSED ME ON THE CHEEK!

I told her how much I enjoyed the play and what a wonderful performance it was. Now I was annoyed that most of the people in line had left, so they couldn't see how important I was.

"Thank you! I'm so glad you came! You should've told me you were coming."

"I know," I said, "I just wasn't sure how to reach you."

"You could've left a message with the box office. Anyway, since I'm almost done here, would you like to walk me back to my hotel? I'm staying at the Plaza until a sublet comes through."

"Sure. I'd love to," I said.

Now I was REALLY feeling like a big shot.

So I stood to the side and waited with bloated head for the rest of the autograph seekers to get their little autographs. And finally she was free to go.

The night was warm, the air was clean, and I couldn't help feeling like it was good to be alive as I walked up Broadway with this woman who had stolen away the love of my life, but what the hell, she was famous.

"My play must seem like a long time ago," I said, "considering the changes in your life."

"Another lifetime. Those were the days, huh?"

"Those days are still pretty much the same for me now. Not much has changed."

"You're still writing plays?"

"Yes."

"Good," she said, "because you're such a good writer."

"Thanks."

I didn't mention that I had a play up right then at the Matrix Theater. Even though something was better than nothing, it would sound too god-awful pitiful compared to Broadway.

"*Til Death Do Us Part* deserves to be done again," she said. "Someone should do it Off Broadway."

"Thanks," I said.

I didn't mention not seeing it listed in her credits. I didn't mention that she never did like the ending with the "ghost." I didn't mention that she in fact had the power to get it done *on* Broadway if she would just commit to doing the part.

"Have you seen Peter recently?" she asked.

"No," I lied.

"That's too bad. He liked you."

"You think so?"

"And you liked him."

"He was okay."

She laughed and shook her head and it suddenly felt like no time had passed, and we could step right back into being like we used to be with each other. "You are such a bad actress," she said. "The only person you're fooling is yourself."

"Well it doesn't matter, anyway," I said. "I thought he wanted me. And you proved me wrong."

We had reached The Plaza. And we were standing in front of the entrance, which was surrounded by uniformed bellhops and hotel guests getting in and out of cabs. I felt sorry to have to say good-bye. I knew she probably had all sorts of interesting anecdotes about Hollywood, and there were all sorts of things I needed to know about her like was she or was she not romantically involved with George Clooney like they said on Access Hollywood?

"I'd invite you out for a piece of cake," she said, "but my agent has me on this onerous diet."

I loved the idea of eating cake with her again. I loved how being around her made me feel a little like I was with my sister again. I didn't want to let her go.

"So what's it like?" I asked.

"What's what like?"

"The whole star thing."

"I hate it. I want my privacy back."

"I don't believe you."

"Nobody does. Except my lover." She gave me a little smile then, and a wink. "She's waiting for me upstairs."

"Oh," I said. And smiled back. No wonder. "Then I won't keep you."

"You know, Jennifer . . ."

"What?"

For a fleeting moment I thought she might say something about our own "sexual encounter." My "rejection" of her. How she was still attracted to me, and if I ever wanted to give her a call because the woman upstairs was getting on her nerves . . . (Funny how durable the ego can be even when you have low self-esteem.)

"I always hoped," she said, "that you and Peter would find your way to each other. I felt bad that I interfered."

"It wasn't your fault," I said, thinking that it was. "It just wasn't meant to be."

"I'm not sure. Because . . ."—she hesitated—"that day I walked out on rehearsal . . . and you said he wanted you and not me . . . When Peter called that night to talk about the play, I asked him out for dinner. And I made a move on him. And you were right, you know. He told me he was into you."

"He did?"

"And I told him not to waste his time, because you weren't into him. Which is what you always said, not that I believed it. So he was bummed out, and then I took advantage."

"So he succumbed to you on the rebound?"

"Something like that. I just . . . when I see something I want, I tend to go after it. And you . . ."

"Don't step on everyone who gets in my way?"

"Right. Well. I'm sorry."

"So maybe you'd like to make it up to me."

"Oh, I haven't seen Peter in ages."

"But you could do something about my play."

"Your play?" she said, as if she had no idea what I was getting at.

"You could do another production of *Til Death Do Us Part*. Because," I made myself continue, "I do agree it never did get the production it deserved. And you certainly have the pull now . . . I mean, I know you're incredibly busy but maybe you could fit it into your schedule somehow, because you really were wonderful in the part of Julia."

"Oh. That's so sweet of you," she gushed a bit too much. "Thank you so much for saying that. But don't you think I'm too old to play Julia now?"

"No. She's supposed to be in her twenties . . ."

"Early twenties . . ."

"Mid twenties . . . late twenties . . ." (Kelly's exact age was a mystery.) "It doesn't really matter."

"Well . . . it *is* a wonderful play," she said. "Why don't you send it to me, and I'll read it again. And anything else you've written since then. Does that sound good?"

"That sounds great," I said. It sounded like a brush-off, but at least I had asked. I didn't have to go through the rest of my life annoyed with myself for not asking.

"Well . . . it's wonderful to see you, Jennifer."

"And it's great to see you. Congratulations on all your success. It's wonderful."

"Thanks."

We kissed cheeks good-bye. And I watched, along with the bellhop, as she went inside the hotel. Then he looked back at me and our eyes met, and he smiled. Very impressed. I smiled back. Let him be impressed, I thought. Maybe it wasn't a brush-off. Maybe she would do what she said. But I knew, as I headed west on Central Park South towards home, it was more likely I would never hear from her again.

Chapter
15

The next day, I picked up the phone. Don't think, I told myself, don't feel. Just act. I dialed Peter's number and got his machine. I didn't hang up.

"Hi Peter. It's Jennifer. It was nice seeing you at my play. Can you give me a call? My number is still the same. Thanks. Bye."

I hung up in a sweat, pumped with adrenaline, and had to go on a walk to work it out of my system.

The next afternoon the phone rang. I was watching *All My Children* and was very involved in a confrontation between Erica (the aging bitch) and Greenlee (the up-and-coming bitch) so I almost didn't pick up the phone, but then I was glad I did.

"Hello?

"Hi."

"Peter."

"I hope I'm not interrupting your writing."

"Oh no, it's fine," I said, stretching the cord of the phone so that I could reach the TV and turn the sound off.

"I got your message," he said.

"Yes. Thanks for calling back."

"What's up?"

I paused. This was the moment. "Would you be interested in having dinner with me tomorrow night?"

I screwed up my face as if bracing for a collision.

"Sure," he said.

"Great." I relaxed my face.

"Is there anywhere you have in mind?"

"Not especially."

"Because I've heard there's a cafe in Riverside Park."

"Riverside Park?" I didn't tell him I'd never been in that park.

"It's supposed to be nice. Why don't we meet on Seventy-second by the statue of Eleanor Roosevelt. We'll find it together."

"Okay. Around six?"

"Great," he said. "See you there."

I hung up. And turned off the TV. I had more important things to do now. Like figure out what I was going to wear.

As I went through my closet and decided that everything I owned was ugly and unflattering, I tried to think about how I was going to approach him. Emotionally. Because it didn't feel simple in my mind. I mean, he did sleep with Kelly. And they had continued to sleep together for the run of my play and an unknown amount of time after that. And sure, maybe he'd been under the impression that I didn't want him. And maybe I hadn't done enough to let him know I did. But still, I kept thinking as I took out some clothes to try on, that didn't mean he had to go and have such a good time with her!

I found my favorite pair of black capris on a hook underneath three sweaters and closed my closet door and tried to push all those jealous feelings to the back of my mind. The capris were wrinkled and there was a food stain on the knee.

They would have to be dry-cleaned. That meant a one-day rush-job place where they'd charge a million dollars. Oh well. No matter how much this was going to cost me, I had to look good.

Peter was there waiting for me, and my breath drew in a little at his tall leanness. He kissed my cheek when he greeted me.

"You look very nice," he said.

I was wearing a new indigo blue tank top with spaghetti straps that was decorated with a fringe of black beads along the bottom hem. I'd bought it at H & M after taking the capris to the dry cleaners. I convinced myself to buy it by telling myself it was something Kelly might wear. Meaning it was a little tighter and sexier than what I usually wore.

"Thank you," I said. "You cut your hair."

"Just this morning as a matter of fact."

I wondered if he'd done it in anticipation of seeing me.

"It looks nice."

"Thank you."

Though I did miss his curls. If something did develop between us, I'd have to work on that.

"Beautiful day, huh," he said.

"Yeah, it's nice." It was perfect. The sun was out and it wasn't too humid.

We started down the path into the park. There was a big fenced-in area where some dogs were having the time of their lives running around unleashed with their tongues hanging out.

"I hope you don't mind," he said, "that I came to your play even though you asked me not to."

"I suppose I'll forgive you eventually."

We went on a path that led us down through a tunnel that

went under the West Side Highway to a long stone staircase that took us down to a lower path that went by a field where some kids were playing baseball by a promenade along the river.

"I can't believe this is here, right in the middle of New York City," I said. "It's like an alternative reality."

"Yeah. I don't get into the park as often as I should."

"I never do. I always think I'm going to get disoriented and end up in Long Island City."

"You can't get lost in Riverside. It's too narrow. You've got the river on one side and the city on the other."

"That's true." I decided that for a park, this one wasn't that bad.

We walked along the promenade and he asked how my play was going at the Matrix. "Audiences seem to like it. But you know how it is. We haven't had any reviews, so it's tough getting audiences. We've been having a lot of nights where it's half empty."

"You mean half full."

"Right."

We paused at the railing and looked out over the water. New Jersey was on the other side. Even so, it was nice. There were high-rises and some strings of houses, but it wasn't so developed that you couldn't get a sense of the palisades rising on the other side.

"Whenever I come here," Peter said, "I ask myself why I don't come more often."

"Now that I'm here," I said, "I'm amazed I've never been."

We stood there taking it all in.

And unpleasant thoughts entered my mind.

I wanted some kind of reassurance from him about Kelly so I could put my hurt feelings to rest. But I didn't want to spoil things by bringing her up. So I told myself to forget about it.

We continued on down the promenade until we reached the restaurant. It was crowded with people dining at white metal tables under colored umbrellas. People idling in the sun as if they were at some nice resort on the French Riviera and not just the Hudson River which everyone knows is polluted with sewage and dead bodies. We found an empty table and joined everyone else pretending to be on the Riviera.

We both ordered "Boat Basin Salads." I put on my sunglasses as the sun set before our eyes. When the salads came, I did my best to get the rather large pieces of lettuce into my mouth without looking like a slob. It wasn't until we were done eating that I asked him, "Can I ask you something?"

"Sure."

"I know that I was giving off some mixed messages . . . and it's not surprising that you would be attracted to Kelly . . ."

"I don't know why I let myself get involved with her," he interrupted. "It was a mistake."

Good, I thought. Leave it at that. That was all that needed to be said.

"How long did it last," I asked. "After the play closed?"

"When she started rehearsals for Rocco's production. That's when she became impossible."

"So a few months?"

"Not that long. I don't know." He sounded annoyed, but I wasn't sure if it was with himself or me. "I don't remember."

I took a sip of water. Some people in a boat sailed by. I don't understand people who go on boats. They always seem to be having a good time. Or they want everyone to think they're having a good time just because they're in a dumb boat.

"I don't suppose it makes much difference to you," he went on, "but she told me you didn't find me attractive. So when she told me that . . ."

"I didn't tell her that."

He was silent for a few moments. "Well. I'm sorry," he repeated. "I never meant to hurt you."

"She is a very sexy woman," I added unnecessarily.

"Yes."

"And we certainly aren't the only people in the world who think so," I added even more unnecessarily.

"Not by a long shot," he agreed.

As the waitress cleared our plates, I wondered if we might go to a movie together or something. Neither of us had mentioned any plans beyond dinner. We argued over who was going to pay the bill. I said I should pay because I asked him out. He wouldn't let me. Finally, I agreed to let him pay if I could pay the next time. He agreed, and we started walking back along the promenade.

"So," Peter said. "I hope everything is all cleared up as far as Kelly is concerned."

"Yes," I said, dodging a tall man with hairy legs who was roller blading right towards me.

"Because I was starting to think I made a mistake."

"What do you mean?"

"I went to the Helen Hayes Theater and bought tickets for *Betrayal* tonight. I thought we might go."

"Really?" I felt very unpleasantly annoyed.

"Was it a bad idea? The day I ran into you on the street, I had the impression you wanted to go."

I was too embarrassed to tell him I already had gone.

"No. I don't really want to." And I didn't. Not that night. Not with him.

"It was a bad idea," he said. "Forget about it."

"What will you do with the tickets?"

"I don't know."

"I'm sure they were expensive."

"They weren't cheap."

"You can't just throw them out."

"I'll figure something out."

"You must want to see it."

"Well. I suppose I could go by myself. I can sell the other one at the theater."

Instead of doing something with me? That was *really* annoying. And the idea of him sitting there by himself gaping at her like an adoring fan.

Like I had.

Wasn't anyone immune?

We walked up out of the park without speaking. When we reached Riverside Drive he asked me what I wanted to do.

"I don't know," I said. All I did know, was I wanted him to tell me that he had no desire to see Kelly in *Betrayal* and she was an overrated actress and he'd much rather spend the evening apologizing to me for ever having sex with her.

"Well," he said, "I am curious to see it."

"Then you should go."

"Are you sure?"

"Yes."

"I'll take the train downtown with you then."

"Okay."

We walked over to subway station together. "Front row mezzanine," he tried to tempt me once more. "You sure you don't want to go?"

"No thanks."

We descended into the station. As we stood on the platform I could see the headlights of a train approaching. I realized that if he stayed to talk to Kelly after the show, she would tell him I saw her. That would be embarrassing. I panicked. "Maybe it would be better . . ." I began, but I was drowned out by the supersonic, ear-splitting screech of the train as it braked to a stop.

We squeezed onto the train, which was packed. "Did you say something?!" he asked as we both held onto a pole. It was so noisy and crowded. I couldn't raise my voice above all these people out for a good time. I wasn't sure what I would say, anyway. I smiled and shook my head.

As we pulled into the Fiftieth Street station, he raised his voice above the racket and said, "I'm glad we did this!"

"Me too! Have fun at the show!"

"Thanks!"

When I got out of the subway, I went into the corner deli and bought a huge bag of low-fat potato chips and a two-liter bottle of diet root beer. I went home and turned on the TV. There was an old movie on—Cary Grant and Audrey Hepburn in *Charade*. I'd seen it before, but I remembered it was good. A commercial came on, and there she was. Kelly Cavanna in an ad for *Betrayal* that had little clips of her performance. A voiceover quoted her rave review in the *Times*. Play extended, they said. Due to popular demand.

Well, I thought to myself, I have my own play to go to. I could go and watch my own play. Maybe I had disdained the Matrix Theater, but tonight I was grateful they would have me. I turned off the TV and headed back out.

I arrived at the theater just as everyone was filing in after intermission and took a seat in the back row. It was a good Saturday night audience thank god, and the laughter was healthy. I let that wonderful sound enter my pores like medicine. Even if my audience had to sit in the stinky Matrix Theater, it was enjoying itself as much as the people watching *Betrayal* and at a fraction of the price.

But it was hard sitting through my ending. The fake me did what the real me couldn't.

Gabrielle: *"The truth is . . ."*

Paul: *"Yes?"*

Gabrielle: *"I'm in love with you, Paul. I've been in love with you since the day we met. And you interviewed me. And I thought you weren't going to give me the job, but then you did . . ."*

When Paul and Gabrielle kissed and the audience applauded, I felt disgusted with myself. Maybe I'd succeeded in getting the characters in my plays to be open with their (my) feelings. But so what? In my own real life, I was still hiding out in the back row.

I watched the actors take their curtain call and knew that I should've told Peter to throw those tickets out and spend the evening with me. Instead, right this very minute, he was probably watching her sign autographs on her fan's Playbills. Maybe she was even signing his: *"Let's go to your place and find out how many orgasms I can have before my next performance, Kelly."* Within minutes they'd be having a passionate make-out session in the backseat of a cab on the way to Peter's apartment. And I would be returning home, once again, alone.

I stood up from my seat and decided to hightail it to the Helen Hayes Theater. It was only about six blocks away, and there was a good chance he was out on the sidewalk waiting for her to come out. I was so intent on snaking through the people from my audience who were taking their own sweet time getting out of the theater that I almost didn't see Peter standing there on the sidewalk.

"Jennifer?"

I turned to the sound of his voice. "Peter. What are you doing here?"

"I called your apartment and there was no answer. I thought you might be here."

"Yeah, I just thought I'd see how it was going."

"And?"

"The lights were on during the curtain call."

"That's good."

"Do you feel like getting a bite to eat?" I ventured.

"That's what I was going to ask you," he said. "I was thinking of this deli on Forty-eighth Street."

"That sounds good."

We walked up Eighth Avenue. I wondered if he'd seen *Betrayal.* Talked to Kelly. I wondered if I was going to be able to say the words I wanted to say.

The deli was crowded from the posttheater crowd, but we still managed to get a nice little table against the wall. A signed headshot of Dustin Hoffman from the 70s hung over the table. Dustin had signed it, "Thanks for the corned beef."

"I'm so starved I want everything," I said, looking at the gigantic menu. "I know. Cheese blintzes. I'm getting that."

I put down my menu. He was looking at me funny. I wondered if Kelly had told him I saw her.

"I just want you to know," he began, "I meant to tell you this afternoon . . . The other week, after I saw the production of your play at the Matrix, I was going to call you."

"Why didn't you?"

"At first I was flattered. I thought it was about you and me. But then when I thought about it, I started to wonder if the part of Paul was based on *Kelly.*"

"Really?!"

"You're not the only person around here who feels insecure."

"You're the one who slept with her," I reminded him.

"Only because you rejected me."

"I didn't reject you."

"You certainly didn't let me know how you felt."

"But neither did you. I mean, you gave up on me so easily and went straight to her."

"She made it easy, I'll admit that. But you have to believe me. She wasn't my first choice."

I felt myself blush.

"Well," I said, staring at a bowl of pickles on the table, "the part of Paul was based on you."

"Really?"

"Yes." I looked up from the pickles. Our eyes met. "When she says she loves him . . . that's what I wanted to say to you. And I do. Love you, I mean."

My heart was having such palpitations I thought it was going to explode and splatter blood all over my menu.

"That's nice to hear," he said, "because that's what I wanted to say to you. And I do. Love you, I mean."

I relaxed. Breathed out. We looked at each other. And I knew. Everything was going to be okay.

The waiter came to take our order. "You know what you want?"

"The young lady will have the cheese blintzes," Peter said, still looking into my eyes, "and I will have a pastrami sandwich on rye."

Pastrami?

"Wait," I said. "Peter?"

"Yes?"

"Are you sure . . . ?"

I hadn't forgotten what he told me years ago. About never eating it since his father died.

"What kind of bread?" the waiter asked.

"An onion roll."

"You know what?" I said. "Cancel my blintz. I'll have pastrami too. Put mine on rye."

The waiter took our menus and left.

"So," I asked, "when did you start eating pastrami again? Or is this the first time?"

"Like a virgin."

"Wow. And . . ." We both looked down at a jar of mustard next to the bowl of pickles. "Are you going to . . . ?"

"Yes," he said, moving it to the center of the table. "My first pastrami sandwich with mustard since my father died. Quite an occasion."

"What made you decide?"

"You."

"Me?"

"Yeah. You inspire me."

"I inspire you?"

I inspired someone?

"You're a very brave person. You let yourself feel," he said, "everything you needed to feel."

I raised my glass of water. "To no more guilt for being alive . . ."

He clinked my glass. "When other people are dead."

And then we were both silent.

And then I had to ask.

"So did you go to *Betrayal?*"

"No."

"No?"

"I gave the tickets to some friends. Now they owe me a favor. It's fine. I'm sure I didn't miss anything."

I refrained from saying that it was really fun seeing Kelly up there on the big stage.

The waiter brought our food, and Peter put a big smear of mustard on his rye bread. I watched as he bit into the sandwich.

"Good?" I asked.

"Excellent," he said between chews.

And I took a bite of mine. I had to get over a slight psychological barrier of my own because usually I get grossed out by deli meat sandwiches. But I had to admit—it tasted really good. And I ate the whole thing, except for the crusts, which I always leave behind.

Even though I was full, when the waiter came to take our plates away and asked if there would be anything else, I said, "I'll have a piece of cheesecake." And then I said, aside, to

Peter, "My sister and I used to get it all the time. We shared because it's so fattening."

The waiter turned to Peter. "For you?"

"Bring an extra fork."

"One cheesecake," the waiter said, and left to get the order.

"You don't have to," I said. "If you'd rather get something else . . ."

"I would be honored to share your cheesecake," Peter said, reaching over and placing a lock of hair behind my ear.

My mouth watered in anticipation. Or should I say salivated.

After dinner, we walked through Times Square. Peter held my hand as we snaked through the hordes of Saturday night partiers. He started to laugh.

"Why are you laughing?"

"I'm just remembering the look on your face opening night, when Kelly grabbed the script out of your hand. I thought you were going to faint right on stage."

"And that amuses you?"

"But you know what? You were good. That was good acting."

"But is it acting," I asked him, "when you're just saying what you feel?"

"Saying what you feel. One of the hardest things to do."

"I feel . . ." I paused. Hesitated. Forged ahead. ". . . like inviting you over to my place."

He looked at me with surprise. "Well," he teased, "it would save me the cab fare home."

"Then I insist." As we made our way down the avenue to my apartment, I wondered if he could tell I had the jitters, like an actress on opening night.

* * *

If I try to describe it, I'm afraid it will just sound like stupid pornography.

Actually, we should all be so lucky.

I guess I just don't want to think about it. The details of what his kiss did to my body. It's like it made my . . . I hate this word . . . cunt . . . I would never use that word but there it is . . . his kiss made it open up . . . like one of those, what do you call them, those things in the ocean, those plants that eat fish that open up and nab a fish as it's going by? This is an inane metaphor, I know, and I am completely incapable of describing this, but it was really like I opened up and wanted to take him in and pull him into me.

And he had me against the door, and he rubbed against me, and I felt his, you know, thing, okay "penis" big and hard against me, and it was HIM! After all this time, it was HIM and ME doing this! And he had me against the door, and his hands cupping my butt . . . bottom . . . ass . . . whatever . . . and he was pressing me up and into him, his lips all warm and soft.

This is horrible. Now I'm sounding like a Harlequin Romance.

I actually read a Harlequin Romance once and it wasn't that bad.

Well, it was pretty bad. But I read it.

In any case . . .

I wish I could say we became mad, passionate lovers and had incredibly hot sex without using birth control in every position imaginable over and over again until we were utterly exhausted.

But it wasn't like that.

I opened the door with shaking hands. Shaking all over, my body literally shaking. And we immediately made our way to the bed.

And one by one, every piece of our respective pieces of clothing were removed.

And . . .

I think I have to stop now. I think I should end this right here. I probably should've ended this before I got this far, because now I don't want to finish. But this would not make a very satisfying ending right here.

I think I need to go get a cup of tea.

Okay, I'm back. I made some tea, and I inhaled about twenty honey roasted peanuts while I waited for the water to boil.

So anyway. This is the thing. The final embarrassing thing.

While we made love, I thought about Peter and me on a bed—center stage—making love. Having quite passionate, noisy bump and grind sex. And the audience? Sold out. Completely full. Eyes riveted on us. And the best part was . . . they were all *paying* audience. No comps. No friends. No relatives. Not even Kelly or Diana. Just total strangers. And they weren't laughing at me or thinking I looked ridiculous or taunting me or even encouraging me for being carnal. They were totally silent and transfixed and turned on by my incredible performance.

And it was that night, with Peter, that I had, in the presence of another person, an orgasm. Another word I hate, by the way.

The way it rhymes with spasm. Makes me think of epileptic fits. Anyway, I had it. I know, I know. Big deal. At my age, nothing to write home about, that's for sure. And it wasn't even, like, an incredible orgasm. Just a modest one. But I had it. With him.

And it was a beginning.